The Warning

Also by Sophie Hannah

The Warning

A Short Story

SOPHIE HANNAH

WITNESS
IMPULSE
An Imprint of HarperCollinsPublishers

This work was previously published in 2015 by Hodder Paperbacks in the UK under the title *Pictures or it Didn't Happen*.

Excerpt from *Woman with a Secret* copyright © 2015 by Sophie Hannah

EPub Edition JUNE 2015 ISBN: 9780062428844
Print Edition ISBN: 9780062428851

10 9 8 7 6 5 4 3 2 1

Chapter 1

"I DON'T BELIEVE this, Mum!" Freya wails at me. "Please say you're joking!"

I am not joking. She must be able to see that from my face.

No, no, no.

It can't be true. I can't have screwed up so disastrously.

Except I have. I've forgotten the music for Freya's audition. *No, no, no, no, no. . .*

I didn't exactly forget it. Not completely. I remembered to put it in the car. Then, stupidly—so stupid that I can't actually believe it—I left it there. *I left it in the fucking car.* Now, when I urgently need it to be safely inside my bag, it's in the Grand Arcade car park.

I'm an idiot. Worse than an idiot. I am every bad thing.

A vicious, skin-piercing wind whips around my head. My hair hits my face like lashes from a cold whip. Cambridge is always either much warmer than everywhere else or much colder. Today, it's imitating a Siberian winter.

"What are we going to do?" Freya demands. Her eyes are wide with panic. I know what she's hoping for: any answer that isn't, "There's nothing we can do. It's too late." She's been practicing her audition song for weeks—recording herself, then listening carefully to each recorded version, making notes on how to improve her vocal technique.

Freya is nine. She's known since the age of five that she wants to be a singer. This will be the first time she puts her voice to the test. I'm terrified of how crushed she'll be if she fails. "I *cannot* mess this up, Mum," she's been saying every five minutes since she woke up this morning. "I *have* to get in. They *have* to say yes."

Now, thanks to me, she's going to miss her chance to try. I've failed on her behalf. She can't audition without her music, which her brainless mother has left in the bloody, fucking car. The only thing that mattered, the one crucial thing...

My teeth are chattering from the cold. At the same time, my neck is too hot beneath my poncho. I wonder if I'm about to faint.

"Mum!" Freya's voice pulls me back. "What are we going to *do*?"

Think, Chloe. Quickly. You have to solve this problem, and the seconds are ticking by...

It's like a math problem from one of Freya's homework sheets. I look at my watch. We're about ten minutes away from where the auditions are happening. It would take us ten minutes to walk back to the car park—ten minutes in the opposite direction. Freya's audition is in twelve minutes.

"We'll have to run back to the car and get the music!" she says, blinking hard, trying not to cry. "Come on! Don't just stand there!"

"There's no time, Freya. Unless we suddenly both learn to fly, we won't make it. We'll miss your slot." My heart thumps dizzying beats in my mouth. I tell myself that this isn't a life-or-death emergency. It feels like one.

I look at my watch again, desperately hoping time will have started to race backward. It hasn't.

"We can't go back, okay?" I say, struggling to stay calm.

"We *have* to!"

"We *can't*! We only have twelve minutes! It's not long enough. You read the letter: anyone who misses their allotted time—tough luck, they're out."

People are staring at us as we stand on Bridge Street shouting at each other. "Freya, listen. I know this feels like a disaster, but—"

"It *is* a disaster! How can I sing without my music?"

"You'll have to manage. Look, we'll pick another song—one that whoever's playing the piano will definitely know. It's not ideal, but—"

"Like what?" Freya demands. "What song?"

"I don't know! 'Happy Birthday To You,' or . . ."

"No way." My daughter's face hardens. I feel like the worst kind of traitor. "Do you even *know* how embarrassing that would be, Mum? Happy *Birthday*? No! I can't *believe* you left the music in the car! *Why* did I trust you? Give me your keys!" She holds out her hand. "Without you slowing me down, I can run back to the car and still get to the audition by half past."

"No way! You absolutely could not. And anyway—"

"Give me the car keys, Mum!"

"Freya, there's no way I'm letting you run through Cambridge on your own—"

"Give *me* the car keys," a man's voice says firmly, cutting through my frantic babbling. "I'll go."

I turn to face him. He's tall and thin, with floppy, straight, dark brown hair and brown eyes, but I don't notice any of that at first. I'm too busy staring at his bike.

If only I had a bike right now . . . But no, that still wouldn't work. I couldn't leave Freya alone in the center of Cambridge. If she were just a few years older . . . but she isn't. She's nine.

"Obviously, I kind of overheard," says the dark-haired man. "As did all of Cambridge, and indeed most of Peterborough." He smiles to let me know he's teasing me in a friendly way. "Where have you parked, and where are you headed? I'll get the music there in time or die trying." He makes an exaggerated comic "death-throes" face at Freya, who looks up at me hopefully.

"Never trust a stranger," the man tells her solemnly. "Apart from when you've got an important audition—right, young lady?"

"Right," Freya agrees, and I'm startled by the passion in her voice.

There is a cluster of about ten people standing nearby, outside Galleria, staring at us—watching the drama unfold, wondering if I'll say yes or no. Why do they care? It's not a marriage proposal, for God's sake.

My head fills with a muddled jumble of words: *only chance . . . bike . . . fast . . . yes, that'll work . . . he seems nice . . . could be anyone, though . . . might steal car.*

Instead of giving him my keys, I could ask to borrow his bike. I'd have to ask him to wait with Freya, though, which is unthinkable. I'd sooner risk my Volvo than my child.

As if he can read my mind, the man says, "I'll be quicker than you. I'm the Lance Armstrong of Cambridge. Actually, these days I'm probably faster. Since he gave up drugs, poor old Lance can barely wheel his bike alongside him as far as the post office. I've heard there's wheezing involved."

I can't help smiling at his absurd joke. Offhand, I can't remember a time when anyone—friend, relative, or stranger—has tried so hard to make me laugh and, at the same time, solve a problem for me.

He holds out his hand for my car keys.

I give them to him. A voice in my head whispers, "Most people wouldn't do this," but the whisper isn't loud enough to stop me.

Sod it. He's our only hope of getting Freya's sheet music to the audition on time. Whatever happens—even if this stranger steals my battered old Volvo and I never see him or it again—Freya will know that I did everything I could. That I took a risk to help her.

"Nice one, Mum," she breathes. Her approving smile tells me I've made the right choice. Not necessarily the most sensible choice, but the right one.

"Grand Arcade car park, level two," I say too fast. My words trip over themselves. Even with a bike on our side, we can't afford to waste a second. "Silver Volvo S60, MM02 OXY. On the backseat there's some sheet music for a song, 'The Ash Grove.' "

"And I'm bringing it to . . . ?"

"Brooking Hall, next to—"

"I know it." He mounts his bike, winks at Freya and cycles away at speed. Dangerously fast. Maybe he wasn't kidding when he said he'd die trying. I watch him disappear, his black overcoat flying out behind him like a cape—the kind a superhero might wear.

"Come on, Mum!" Freya grabs my arm and starts to drag me along the street. Before too long, frustrated by my slowness, she drops my sleeve and marches on ahead.

I hurry to catch up with her, stunned by what I've just done. I've given my car keys to a man I don't know at all. What kind of crazy fool am I? I didn't even ask his name, didn't get his mobile phone number . . . What will Lorna say when I tell her?

I know exactly what she'll say. She might be my oldest and most loyal friend, but she also enjoys insulting me when she thinks I deserve it. "This is typical of you, Chloe." She'll sigh. "You're so naïve! Why would a total stranger put himself out to help you? You deserve to have your car nicked."

"Darling, don't get your hopes up, okay?" I pant at Freya, out of breath from walking too fast. "He might not get there in time. He might not turn up at all."

"Yes, he will," she insists. "Stop being so negative!"

We arrive at the hall with one minute to spare. A woman with greasy skin and a hole in her tights snaps in my face, "I'm sorry, we're running late!" She's carrying a beige clipboard under her arm. There are chunks missing out of its side, as if it's been nibbled by an animal.

Running late. I let the words sink in. Of course: we're not allowed to be late, but they, the people with all the power, can keep us hanging around as long as they like.

No need for all my panic. No need to hand over my car keys to a total stranger.

"Sit over there," Clipboard Woman barks at me, pointing to a row of chairs that other people are already sitting in. She doesn't even look at Freya. "We'll call your name when we're ready for you. I'm SORRY, we're running late . . ." she snarls at the mother and son who have just walked in behind us. They both flinch. Is there any need for her to bellow at people?

Still. Thank God for this delay. The man with the bike is not here yet.

Of course he isn't, fool. He'll be halfway to London by now—cruising along the M11 in your Volvo, laughing his head off at your stupidity.

"This is ridiculous," a tired-looking bald man says to the girl sitting next to him. I assume she's his daughter. She has serious braces on her teeth. They look painful. "You were supposed to be in a half hour ago. I'm not spending the whole day sitting here."

I look at my watch. Eleven thirty-two. Freya's audition was meant to start two minutes ago. I also don't want to wait forever. On the other hand, I would sincerely like to get my car keys back.

If he was planning to bring them back, he'd be here by now . . .

I hear singing in the distance. Then louder, closer. Not a child's voice, though—a man's, coming from behind me. I know the song painfully well: "The Ash Grove." Freya's audition song, the one she's been practicing for so long.

"Down yonder green valley where streamlets meander,
When twilight is fading, I pensively rove . . ."

I spin round. It's him. *Thank you, Lord.* He's singing at me, with a pleased-as-Punch grin on his face. It's a bit embarrassing in front of all these people.

I want to text Lorna to report that a handsome stranger is singing to me in public. I know what she'd text back: "Pictures or it didn't happen." She always demands proof of everything.

Freya gets straight down to business. "Did you get my music?" she asks.

The dark-haired man matches her solemn expression with one of his own as he hands over the sheets of paper. "Mission successfully accomplished, Your Highness. I pensively roved, I got your music. I even locked the car, so no need to worry about local vagrants hosting a party in it. That happened to my friend Keiran a couple of weeks ago. He came back to find empty cider bottles and burger wrappers all over the backseat of his hundred-grand BMW convertible. He was not amused. So . . . what are you auditioning *for*?" our rescuer asks Freya. "I hope it's going to propel you to superstardom, whatever it is."

"Thank you *so* much," I say, finding my voice at last. I must stop staring at him like someone who has seen a strange vision. I still can't quite believe he did this huge favor for us, with no ulterior motive. He honestly wanted to help. Is anybody really so kind and selfless?

"She's auditioning for the chorus of *Joseph and his Dreamcoat*," I say. "Only thanks to your help. If it weren't for you, we'd be trudging home in tears right now, so . . . thank you. I can't tell you how grateful I am."

I'm in danger of crying. How silly. Anyone would think no one had ever been kind to me before. I blink frantically.

"You're welcome, ma'am."

Ma'am?

Right. That's the worst fake American accent I've ever heard. And . . . oh, my God, now he's saluting me.

"*Joseph and His Dreamcoat*?" he says, frowning. "Last I heard, it was called *Joseph and His Amazing Technicolor Dreamcoat*. Have they dropped the 'Amazing Technicolor' part?"

"No," I tell him. "I just couldn't be bothered to say it."

"How very maverick of you. While you're at it, there are probably some words in the musical itself that could do with a trim. I saw it when I was a teenager—at the Palace Theater in Manchester, my hometown—and still vividly remember the lyrics of the song about Pharaoh: 'No one had rights or a vote but the king / In fact you might say he was *fairly right wing.'* Awful, just awful!" He sounds very jolly about it, as if awfulness is one of his favorite things.

"The tunes are brilliant," says Freya. "It's a musical. The music's more important than the words."

"I'm not sure I'd agree, Your Highness. When the words are *that* bad . . . Still, only one thing really matters, and that's launching your career as one of the great divas of our time. Am I right?"

"Um . . ." Freya looks at me, unsure what to say.

"And what's all this chorus nonsense?" our new friend goes on. "You should be going for the main part."

"The main part's Joseph," says Freya, with a trace of impatience in her voice. "I'm a girl."

"Well, girl or not, I think you'd make a great Joseph. Or a great Technicolor Dreamcoat—one or the other. And don't dare to tell me you're not a coat! Enough of this humility!"

Freya laughs and blushes. I laugh too. I can't help it.

"Okay, ladies, well . . . I'd better be on my way. Knock 'em dead. Here are your car keys. Oh, hold on . . ." Instead of my keys, he pulls an iPhone out of his pocket. It's ringing. His ringtone is "The Real Slim Shady" by Eminem, which surprises me. He's wearing a smart gray suit, with red bicycle clips around the bottoms of his trousers. Not a man who looks as if he'd be into rap music.

He glances at his phone, then puts it to his ear. "Tom Rigby," he says.

Tom Rigby. Tom Rigby. I'm glad I know his name, though I'm not sure why. He's a stranger. In a minute he's going to walk out of here and I'll never see him again.

The conversation he's having is obviously something to do with his work, and makes no sense to me. Something about chips and a database, and payment compliance, whatever that is. I don't think he means the kind of chips you put salt and vinegar on. He keeps mentioning a name: Camiga, or Camigo. Perhaps it's a company name. It sounds like the kind of thing a serious scientific company might call itself. Very different from my own tiny business, Danglies—but then I work alone, make earrings and earn hardly any money.

When he's finished talking, Tom Rigby stuffs his phone back into his pocket and pulls out my car keys. His hand touches mine as he passes them to me. "There you go," he says. "Right, I've got to scoot. Best of luck, Freya."

He must have overheard me saying her name when we were shouting on Bridge Street. His tone has changed from teasing to straightforward. Obviously he has finished joking around and wants to get on with the rest of his day.

Which is absolutely fair enough.

"Thank you again!" I call after him as he rides away.

Chapter 2

"CHLOE, FOR GOD'S sake! Freya's a talented singer—of course she got in! What, do you think this Tom Rigby bloke's got magic powers? He hasn't. He's just a charming, handsome man with red bicycle clips. This is Freya's achievement, not his."

It is a week after the *Joseph* auditions. I'm in the Eagle pub on Benet Street, having a drink with my best friend and harshest critic, Lorna Tams. Lorna is 42, ten years older than me. Two years ago, she left her husband, Josh. She has since divorced him, and invented a tagline to describe him: "A nice enough bloke, but not the husband I deserve."

When I first met Lorna, she worked in a brewery. Now's she's given that up and is training to be a Methodist minister. When I asked her about the change of direction, she said, "Beer got boring."

I know next to nothing about the Methodist church. I

hope they like their ministers to dress provocatively and simmer with disdain, or else Lorna won't fit in at all.

"Tom Rigby didn't cast a spell that made the judges say yes to Freya," she says now. "He did you a favor for sure, but he isn't some kind of . . . good luck charm on legs."

Then why do I feel as if that's exactly what he is?

"A hundred and twenty-three children auditioned for the chorus," I tell Lorna. "Only twenty got in. Freya was one of them. I'm not saying it was down to Tom Rigby alone, but . . . there *was* something magical-feeling about the whole experience."

"Magical? You mean you fancied him?"

"No, I didn't," I say indignantly. "I didn't think about him in that way at all."

"Hmm." Lorna narrows her eyes. "All right, then. So we're going to stop talking about him, are we, and talk about your talented daughter instead?"

I bite my lip. Sometimes I wish Lorna weren't as clever as she is. It would make my life a lot easier.

The truth is, I am not quite ready to forget all about Tom Rigby.

"I need to thank him," I say quietly—so quietly that I can hardly hear my own words over the louder voices of the students at the table next to ours. I don't like this part of the Eagle. I would prefer to sit in the room to the right of the front door, which is never as noisy as this, but Lorna always insists on sitting in what she calls "the historical part."

"You did thank him," she points out, like a police detective trying to pick holes in a suspect's story. "Profusely, several times, from what you've told me."

"I *said* thank you, yes, but I'd like to thank him properly. He did us such a huge favor."

"Right. By 'thank him properly,' you of course mean hunt him down and force him to marry you?"

"No, I mean I'd like to get him a card, or . . ." I daren't finish my sentence. I stare awkwardly down at the table, too embarrassed to say any more.

"A card *or*?" Lorna laughs. "You're so transparent! A card *or*," she repeats. "You've already got him a present, haven't you? What? Tell me! What did you buy him? Ugh, Chloe, I despair of you. Have you bought anything for your star of a daughter, by the way? The one who actually, y'know, got the part in *Joseph*?"

"Yes. I made her something." I don't feel like telling Lorna that the "something" was a necklace: a tiny opaque glass box on a chain, with a miniature technicolor dreamcoat inside it. It took me four whole days to get it right. It's beautiful, and Freya loves it. If Lorna wants to think I'm neglecting my daughter in favor of a handsome stranger, let her. It will serve her right to be wrong.

"And what did you make for Tom Rigby?" she asks, eyeing me warily.

I feel my face overheat. My present for Tom took me only half a day to make. It was much less intricate: a tiepin. A sequence of musical notes inside a rectangular metal frame. Notes from "The Ash Grove," Freya's audition song.

Down yonder green valley where streamlets meander. . .

"You're too embarrassed to tell me what you've made for him," says Lorna, watching me closely. "This does not bode well. Is it a dildo covered in love hearts?"

I can't be bothered to respond to this insulting suggestion.

"How can you give it to him, anyway? You don't know where to find him."

"I can try. I heard him say the name of a company, when he was talking on his phone. Camigo, or Camiga. Maybe that's where he works. It should be easy enough to find."

Lorna groans into her pint of ginger beer shandy. "You're serious about this, aren't you? You're planning to track him down. Don't. Listen to me, Chloe."

"Do I have a choice?"

"Tom Rigby came to your and Freya's rescue when you needed it. He was the savior of the moment, for twenty minutes one Saturday morning, but the moment passed, as all moments do. You thanked him, and now it's over. You're back to being strangers. All this making him presents and trying to find him, it's not about thanking him properly. Can't you see that? You're craving a repeat performance—more of his magic. You want him to save you again. Maybe for longer this time, right? Maybe forever."

"Lorna, I don't want to marry Tom Rigby. I don't know him."

"You want to get to know him," she says accusingly.

"No! Look, I just don't want to let him disappear with no more than a 'Thank you so much' from me. I want to put myself out for him, like he put himself out for me and Freya. So, yes, I've made him a present," I say defiantly. "Not because

I want him to scoop me up and ride off into the sunset with me, but purely for the sake of doing a nice, generous thing. What's so wrong with that?"

Lorna shakes her head. "You know what? Part of my issue is that this guy sounds too nice. 'Ma'am'? 'Your Highness'? I mean, yuck! Okay, so he didn't steal your wheels—and who can blame him? That Volvo's a rusty old heap of junk—but what if the whole 'Look, I'm giving you back your car keys' thing was a ploy to reel you in?"

This idea is so absurd, it makes me laugh. "Well, then he failed, didn't he? Like you said: as far as he's concerned, he's never going to see me again. And why on earth would he want to 'reel me' anywhere? You think he took one look at me screaming at Freya on Bridge Street and thought, 'That woman looks well-heeled. I'm going to come to her rescue, charm her into marrying me, then murder her and inherit her cash ISA that's worth all of fifteen hundred pounds'?"

"That's true." Lorna casts her disapproving eyes over me. "You don't look as if you've got anything worth inheriting. All right, I'll be blunt. Blunt*er*, I should say. I'm suspicious of Tom Rigby for one reason only: because you're not. Don't be offended, Chloe, but you're a *terrible* judge of character."

"And you're my best friend. So if you're right, what does that say about you?" I sigh. "Is it really so terrible that he called me 'Ma'am' and Freya 'Your Highness'?"

"No," Lorna concedes. "You're right. We have no reason to think Tom Rigby is anything but lovely." She leans both her elbows on the table and glares at me. "That's why he doesn't deserve to be psycho-stalked by you. He did you a favor—great!—and then he said good-bye and walked away. Did he ask for your number? No. Did he suggest meeting again? No. So give the poor man a break and *leave him alone*, Chloe."

Chapter 3

"USELESS GOOGLE!" I mutter at my computer screen later that same night. It's nearly 1 A.M. I really ought to get some sleep, but I'm too stubborn. I refuse to go to bed disappointed. And since Freya is at my mum and dad's until lunchtime tomorrow, it's the perfect chance for me to do some research.

I can't find any company called Camigo or Camiga that looks as if Tom Rigby might work for it. There's Camigo Media, but they make games apps for mobile phones. I'm pretty sure that wasn't what Tom's business call was about. He was discussing a bank, I think. He didn't say the word *bank*, but I had the impression that he worked with money.

The only Tom Rigbys and Thomas Rigbys in Cambridge that I've managed to find online are definitely not him. One is too old. Another has the wrong face in his LinkedIn photo.

Where do I go from here? What else can I search for? "Tom Rigby red bicycle clips"? "Tom Rigby sings 'The Ash Grove'"?

Absurd.

I type "Dr. T Rigby" into the search box and find a Dr. Thomas Rigby in North Carolina, an expert in crop science. He's not the man I'm looking for, and therefore, momentarily, I hate him.

I'm never going to find my Tom Rigby. Why is that such an unbearable prospect? There must be something wrong with me. Lorna was right. I must be crazier than even she suspects, to allow a complete and utter stranger to become so important to me.

A horrible thought occurs to me: what if that's not his name? What if he was talking about somebody else called Tom Rigby, and I misunderstood?

No, that's impossible. He said it in a "My name is . . ." kind of way. Introducing himself. I was in no doubt at the time.

My phone buzzes on the table next to me, making me jump. It's Lorna. She has texted, "Don't Google him!"

I text back, "I can't find him anyway."

"Seriously?" she replies. "I found him in 30 secs. Which I KNOW I SHOULD NOT TELL YOU!"

I grab my phone and ring her, my hands shaking. This had better not be a joke.

I wait and wait. *Come on, Lorna. I know your phone's in your hand.*

When she finally picks up, she says drily, "My desire to show off was stronger than my wish to protect you from making a tit of yourself. What can I say? I'm a flawed human being."

"Tell me," I say.

She sighs. "Draw breath first, and let's go over the pros and cons. Chloe, I really think—"

"Tell me!"

"Will you listen to the desperation in your voice?"

"Yeah—desperation not to be toyed with by my sadistic so-called friend. You have the information I want, and you're dangling it in front of me like bait. Stop dicking around and *tell me*, so that I can go to bed."

"Ha! Like you're going to put your pajamas on and drift off to the Land of Nod as soon as you know. Bollocks! You'll be up all night Googling this guy, soon as I've told you who he is."

"Lorna—"

"All right, give me a chance! His name isn't Tom Rigby, R-I-G-B-Y. It's Tom Rigbey with an 'e'. R-I-G-B-E-Y. He's the CSO of a company called CamEgo—one word, capital C, capital E, ego as in *egotist*. Now let me try to describe what they do, without falling asleep, it sounds so dull. They design personal identification software that facilitates payment compliance in the financial sector, globally. Before you ask, I haven't a clue what that means."

"But CSO, that's—"

"Car keys and songs officer," Lorna fires back.

"Chief something, isn't it?'

"Chief scientific officer. He's a smart cookie, is Tom Rigbey."

I frown. That's strange. He didn't look like a boss or manager of anything. He looked too young, for a start—about my age. And . . . wouldn't a chief scientific officer need to behave less frivolously in public places?

"Chloe? Do *not* go to CamEgo's offices and ambush him. And—since you'll ignore that—ring me as soon as you have. I want all the gossip."

Chapter 4

I ARRIVE AT CamEgo's offices at nine o'clock sharp on Monday morning—more punctual, probably, than most of the firm's employees. The office building that houses Tom Rigbey's company is as glossy and shiny as I imagined it would be. It's one of the newly built ones on Brooklands Avenue, close to the Botanic Gardens. CamEgo occupies the top three floors, and I'm waiting on the lowest of these, in reception.

There are two women behind the desk, one in her late fifties and the other in her early twenties. Both are wearing white blouses, black skirts, and CamEgo badges with their names on. Should I approach Nadine Caspian or Rukia Yunis, if I have a choice? Both are currently dealing with other people. I hope one conversation finishes before the other, so that I don't have to choose.

I've worked out what I'll say. I don't want or need to see

Tom Rigbey—that would be too awkward and embarrassing—so I'll simply ask if I can leave the gift bag I've brought, and will they make sure to deliver it safely to him?

As well as the "Ash Grove" tiepin, I've written a note and put it in the bag. It's short and to the point: "Thank you for the music (as ABBA might say!) Lots of love, Chloe (and Freya, who got into *Joseph* thanks to you!)." No kisses. Though I couldn't resist writing my email address in the top right-hand corner.

The ABBA joke is not something I'd have put in a note to anyone else, and I'm not sure if it's witty or just annoying. I included it because it popped into my head, and struck me as the kind of silly joke Tom Rigbey might appreciate.

In the first draft of the note, I drew his attention to the musical content of the tiepin, and told him the notes belonged to "The Ash Grove." I wanted to make sure he'd notice. Then, later, I decided it was crass to point it out, so I tore up what I'd written and started from scratch.

Tom will work it out. Chief scientific officers are clever.

Nadine Caspian is free, having sent the man she was dealing with to wait on a red sofa to her left. "Can I help you?" She smiles at me. "Ooh—have you brought me a prezzie? And it isn't even my birthday!"

I make a noise that sounds like laughing, and hope my ABBA joke is less pathetic than that. People who aren't funny shouldn't try to be. Is that what Tom Rigbey will think when he reads my note?

"It's a present, but I'm afraid it's not for you," I say.

"Ah, well—never mind!" She chuckles. "At least you've

left the bag open, so I can have a nosey at it." She peers in. "Hm, a jewelry box. Let me guess: cuff links for the man in your life?"

That's strange. It was going to be cuff links—that was my first idea, before I decided a tiepin would be better. Cuff links seemed too obvious.

Lorna, at this point, would tell Nadine Caspian that the contents of the box in the bag were none of her business. One of her favorite regular rants is a diatribe against people who, under cover of friendliness, poke their noses into your affairs in an unacceptable way: hotel receptionists who say while checking you in, "So, any special plans for this evening, then?" (To which Lorna once replied with a straight face, "Yes, as a matter of fact: I'm meeting my lover and we're going to try anal sex for the first time. Is that the kind of special plan you mean?")

I'm not as brave or outrageous as Lorna, but I have no intention of answering Nadine Caspian's question. Instead, I say, "It's for Tom Rigbey. I believe he works here?"

Nadine's face twitches. She swallows hard. "Tom Rigbey?" Her friendly, open demeanor of a second ago is gone. I heard alarm in her voice when she said his name. Now she's looking at me warily.

"Yes. Isn't he CSO here?" I ask.

Nadine nods. "He's out all day today. London." These are the words I hear, but the message, unmistakably, is "Go away. Get lost." If not something even ruder.

"That's fine," I say. 'I don't need to see him. I just wanted to leave this for him."

The other receptionist, Rukia Yunis, who is now free and listening to our conversation, leans over and says, "Of course. That's no problem at all. If you give it to me, I'll see that Tom gets it."

Our eyes meet and I see an apology in hers. Silently, she seems to be trying to say, "I'm sorry my colleague's acting like an arse."

I hand her the gift bag, thank her, and turn to leave, wondering if Nadine Caspian is in love with Tom Rigbey. Probably. That would explain her sudden shift from far-too-matey to cold and suspicious. She must think I'm some kind of girlfriend. Maybe *she's* his girlfriend, and thinks I'm trying to steal him away.

I'm halfway down the stairs to the floor below when I hear a voice behind me. "Hey! Wait."

I turn. It's her: Nadine. "Sorry if I was a bit off just then," she says.

"It's fine."

"Well, not really. It's not your fault. I just . . ." She sighs. "There you were with a present, and it turns out to be for Tom Rigbey of all people . . ."

I nearly open my mouth to ask, "What do you mean 'of all people'?" but something stops me. I'm not sure I want to hear the answer she'd give me. I haven't chosen to have this conversation. Nadine Caspian followed me. Forced it on me.

She's standing three steps above me on the staircase. It makes me feel trapped and small. I wish we could talk on the same level, but we can hardly stand side by side on one step— they're too narrow.

I can't decide if she's attractive or not. Her hair is nice—dark blond, thick and subtly highlighted. Her face is heart shaped and her features big and doll-like, but with a slightly hardened look to them. She's around my age: early thirties.

"Something tells me you haven't known Tom Rigbey long," she says. "You don't know him well—am I right?"

I nod.

"This is none of my business, but I'll say it anyway. You seem like a lovely person, so go and get your gift bag back off Rukia and give it to someone else, *anyone* else. Have nothing to do with Tom Rigbey. Give him nothing, tell him nothing, trust him not at all. Avoid him like the plague because that's what he is—a plague in human form."

I can hardly breathe. Did she really just say that?

"And no, he hasn't just dumped me, if that's what you're thinking. He's the CSO of the company I work for—I have no personal connection to him—but . . . I know how dangerous he is."

When I find my voice, I say, "Dangerous how?"

"Are you going to take my advice?" Nadine responds with a question. "Are you going to get that gift bag back?"

"I . . . I haven't decided."

"Then I can't talk to you. If you're under his spell, you'll tell him anything I say. Tomorrow morning I'll find myself out of a job."

"No, I . . ." I stop myself because I might. I might tell Tom Rigbey that one of his receptionists is a nosey troublemaker with no respect for other people's boundaries. I liked him, and I don't like Nadine Caspian. "I can't promise anything without knowing what you're talking about," I say.

Am I being stupid? If there's some aspect of Tom Rigbey's character that I need to be warned about, I should find out what it is. "Can you please tell me what you mean?" I ask Nadine.

She shakes her head. "Sorry. Look, it's your life, and none of my business. I should keep my big mouth shut. Please don't tell him I said anything and . . . please forget I did." She looks and sounds scared as she pushes past me and hurries down the stairs. I expected her to go back up to CamEgo's reception, but perhaps she needs to go out and wouldn't have followed me otherwise.

Not telling Tom Rigbey what she said, assuming I ever meet him again, will be easy. It was so horrible, so extreme. Surely undeserved, too. How could anyone, apart from the worst, most sadistic criminals, deserve to be spoken of in such terms? Repeating insults as vicious as that to a man who has only ever been kind to me . . . it's unthinkable. He'd be so hurt.

Forgetting's going to be slightly harder. If Nadine Caspian wanted me to forget, she should have chosen words that wouldn't sit so heavily in my mind.

"Give him nothing, tell him nothing, trust him not at all. Avoid him like the plague because that's what he is—a plague in human form."

Chapter 5

"SO WHAT DID you do?" Lorna is fizzing with excitement. We're in St. John's Chop House having dinner. Several hours have passed since my exchange with Nadine Caspian. I still haven't forgotten what she said.

"I—"

"No, wait, don't tell me. I want to guess." Lorna shovels a forkful of dauphinoise potatoes into her mouth. "You hung around on the stairs for nearly an hour, agonizing about whether to leave the present where it was or go and get it back. Eventually you decided to leave it. Right?"

"No. I went back to reception and asked the other receptionist, Rukia, to give me the gift bag back—"

"Really? Wow, well done!"

"Wait. I didn't take the present away, I just tore the top off my note—the part where I'd put my contact details. I thought that was the perfect compromise: Tom Rigbey gets his thank-you present, which he deserves and which I want him to have, but I haven't given him my email address, so . . . if this Nadine woman's right and he's dangerous . . . well, he's no danger to me, is he? He has no way of getting in touch."

Lorna sighs. "It's a compromise," she says. "I'm not sure I'd call it perfect. You really took the gift bag back, got out the note, tore the top off it, then stuck it back in the bag and gave it back to the receptionist?'

"Yes."

"She must have thought you were a nutter."

"You don't think I did the right thing?"

"No, Chloe. Don't look so rejected. I never think you do the right thing. You're way too soft and soppy about people."

"What would you have done?"

"First off, I'd have sworn on my honor not to breathe a word of what Nadine told me to Tom Rigbey—that way you might actually have found something out! But even based only on what she said to you, I'd have asked for my prezzie back and scarpered, thankful for a useful warning and a narrow escape."

I stare at my tagliatelli with porcini mushrooms, wondering how long it will be before Lorna orders me to eat it, and whether I'll admit to having lost my appetite or force it down just to shut her up.

"I know what you're thinking, Chloe. You're thinking: 'Mean, nasty Lorna, not giving the benefit of the doubt. What if Nadine is wrong? Wouldn't it be awful and unfair to think badly of Tom Rigbey on the basis of no evidence whatsoever—just hearsay, just someone else's opinion?'"

"Pretty much," I admit.

"You're thinking that I'm thinking, 'There's no smoke without fire.'" Lorna pauses to take a gulp of red wine. "I'm not, though. Sometimes there is smoke without fire—anyone with a brain knows that—so you have to look at the precise nature of the smoke. If Nadine had said, 'You don't want to get involved with Tom Rigbey—he's a real heartbreaker' or something like that, you could safely ignore her—that kind of thing can mean anything. It'd most likely mean he spurned her advances. But 'a plague in human form'? 'Give him nothing, tell him nothing, trust him not at all'? And you said she looked scared? Chloe, come on—that's got to be a warning worth listening to."

"So because she said really terrible things about him, that means she can't be wrong? Why?"

Lorna groans. "How are we still friends?"

"I've no idea." There's no way I'm going to be able to eat anything tonight. I put my fork, empty of food, in my mouth, to create the illusion of eating.

"This isn't a court of law, Chloe. Would Nadine's cryptic warning be enough to get Tom Rigbey locked up forever? No, and nor should it be. It's hearsay. But she works with him. She knows him. You don't. And you have nothing invested in him. If a stranger warns you to steer clear because he's a plague person, why wouldn't you listen to them? Nadine could be wrong—I'm not denying that—but isn't it over-whelmingly more likely that she's right?"

Lorna's questions have stopped sounding like questions, because they aren't. They're conclusions, presented in question form for rhetorical effect. That's why, even though I have answers to each and every one, I don't feel like sharing them with her.

It's not true that I have nothing invested in Tom Rigbey. Not if hope counts as a thing. Hope for what, though? Nothing will happen. Nothing can. I tore my email address off the note. He can't contact me even if he wants to.

Perhaps I ought to try to believe Nadine Caspian, as a consolation. If I can make myself believe I've had a narrow escape . . .

"Eat your pasta, Chloe. Going off your food because Nadine the receptionist might have unfairly maligned your favorite stranger makes no sense. You're living in a complete fantasy world. Whatever your instincts are telling you right now, for God's sake do the opposite. Your judgment's completely askew."

"We don't need to talk about it anymore," I say quietly.

"Good. Fantastic."

"He hasn't got my email or phone number, so. End of story."

"Praise the Lord."

"You're forgetting that I've actually met him. I'm not weighing Nadine's hearsay against nothing, I'm weighing it against my own first-hand experience. Tom Rigbey did something amazing for me and Freya, something no one else would have done. I spoke to him, we chatted. I just don't believe her!"

"Right. Because no manipulative psychopaths know how to chat nicely and fool people. If someone can make a few witty comments about an Andrew Lloyd Webber musical, that proves they're a good person."

"So now you're making him a psychopath?" I snap.

"You know what, Chloe? I *do* believe her. I don't think people say things like that for no reason. I haven't got any proof, but I don't like the sound of Tom Rigbey. Didn't from your first mention of him. All this 'Ma'am' and 'Your Highness' stuff, saluting you, cycling off to the car park for Freya's music as if someone's life depended on it . . . It's too much. Way too much. You said it yourself: 'He did something no one else would have done.' And you didn't ask him to, did you? He overheard, and forced his way in. There was your warning alarm bell, right there—you chose to see it in a positive light because you're naïve, but if you ask me, it's creepy."

"You could be right," I say, not really caring if I mean it or not. A lot of my conversations with Lorna end this way. She loves arguing and could go on all night. I hate it, and usually give in.

I wish I hadn't taken the note out of the gift bag and torn the top off it. I allowed a stranger to scare me. If I'd taken no notice of her, I would now be looking forward to hearing from Tom Rigbey. He'd have been bound to email and thank me. He might have said something about the present and how much he liked it. Whatever he'd have written, I bet it would have made me laugh. Lorna's always telling me that she has my best interests at heart, but most of what she says makes me feel worse, not better.

I wish I'd argued with Nadine Caspian. Tom Rigbey is not a plague in human form. No way. That's too over the top.

I don't buy it. He's sweet, and not dangerous at all. I trusted him with my car keys, and he didn't let me down. I'm the one who's let him down by allowing myself to be scared away by the spiteful insinuations of a stranger.

And now I'll never hear from him again.

Chapter 6

EXCEPT—AND THANK YOU, life, for being so surprising and almost making me believe in God—I do hear from Tom Rigbey again, and in a pleasingly familiar way. Four days after my depressing dinner with Lorna, I'm sitting on a bench on Castle Street, waiting for Freya to emerge from her first *Joseph* rehearsal, when I hear a man's voice singing a song:

"Down yonder green valley, where streamlets meander / When twilight is fading I pensively rove / Or at the bright noontide in solitude wander, / Amid the dark shades of the lonely ash grove; / T was there, while the blackbird was cheerfully singing..."

It's him. I leap to my feet. "Tom Rigbey!" Oops. That was uncool. Too late now to pretend I'm not thrilled to see him. He's got his bike with him. Same red bicycle clips as last time, a black suit, white shirt with thin blue and lilac stripes ...

"Hello, Chloe Whose-Surname-I-Still-Don't-Know-Because-

She-Didn't-Write-It-On-Her-Card." He sounds equally thrilled to see me. My heart is bouncing up and down like an excited toddler in a soft play center ball pit.

"This . . . this is such a coincidence," I stammer.

"Not at all. I hunted you down. I'm pretty ruthless when it comes to stalking people I'm keen on. You don't mind, do you?"

He is obviously joking. I am obviously not going to mention to Lorna that he said it.

"I'm serious," he says. "You wrote in your note that Freya aced the auditions. I found out where and when they were. I figured you'd be exactly where I found you, waiting to collect your talented progeny."

"You were right. Here I am!"

"They don't call me the Talented Mr. Rigbey for nothing. Now, may I draw your attention to this quite exceptionally beautiful tiepin I'm wearing? With what I like to think of as 'our song'"—he mimes quote marks in the air—"'The Ash Grove' contained within it! What an incredibly thoughtful idea. I *love* it—seriously, I can't think of any present I've ever been given before that I've loved anywhere *near* as much. Where did you get it from? I'm guessing the Folk Song Tiepins Warehouse just off the M11, right?"

I giggle. "I made it."

"You *made* it? Wow. You're a genius, Chloe No-Surname."

"No, I'm not. I'm a jewelry maker—that's what I do. And I'm Daniels."

"Daniel's? Who is this Daniel? I'll have him killed."

Another joke not to be repeated to Lorna. Though,

actually, maybe I should tell her. No one who was planning to commit murder would announce it so cheerfully and openly.

"I mean my surname is Daniels. Chloe Daniels."

"Oh. Well, that's a relief. I must admit, I was rather hoping you didn't belong to anybody—apart from Her Highness Freya, that is. But this jewelry business of yours sounds amazing—when did you start it up? What's it called? Is it just you, or do you have a whole team?"

Normally, I like to be asked about my work. It might be a frivolous thing to spend my days doing, but I love it. I look forward to making each new piece, and not many people can say that about their work. And I love having a company, however tiny. I loved choosing its name, all by myself, and not having to consult anyone else.

"It's called Danglies," I say. I can't manage any more words at the moment. My brain is busy doing acrobatics around the idea that Tom Rigbey doesn't want me to belong to anyone. He definitely said that—I didn't imagine it—and there's only one thing it can mean.

"Ah, *voila Mademoiselle Freya*!" Tom exclaims, as she emerges from the rehearsal hall and comes running towards us. I don't speak French, but I'm guessing that he said something like, "Here comes the lovely Freya."

"Congratulations on your successful audition, young lady. Have you been promoted to Pharaoh yet? I'm sure it won't be long."

"What are you doing here?" Freya asks him.

"I wanted to thank your mother for the present she made for me, and she annoyingly withheld her phone number, hoping to shake me off. As a result, I've had no alternative but to become a musical theater groupie."

"I wasn't hoping that at all," I say. "I didn't want you to think I expected a thank-you, that's all."

I've just lied to Tom Rigbey. Nadine Caspian warned me that he was untrustworthy. Maybe she'd have been better off warning him about me. So far in our very short acquaintance, he's been nothing but lovely to me and I've failed him twice—once by taking Nadine's stupid badmouthing too seriously, and now by lying to him.

"I wouldn't have thought that for a moment. And I'm not letting you off the hook, I'm afraid. I think, since you've put me out by making me roam the streets looking for you, I ought to be allowed to take you out for dinner very soon. You and Freya, if she'd like to come too."

"Don't invite me." Freya rolls her eyes. "I mean, thanks, and I get what you're trying to do, but . . . it's silly. You should just invite Mum, on her own. I won't feel left out, abandoned or anything like that."

"Oh." Tom frowns. "Thanks for the tip, remarkably well-adjusted child. See, I feared that not inviting you might have overtones of When-I-marry-your-mother-I-intend-to-keep-you-locked-in-the-cellar. Am I wrong? Because I totally wouldn't keep you locked the cellar. I'm happy to shake on that now if you'd like?"

He extends his hand and Freya shakes it. She says, "I love our cellar. It's where my Xbox is. I'd like to spend more time there—Mum's always dragging me upstairs to do mind-improving things, yawn."

"You should always listen to your mother, if only because she's a jewelry magnate and has access to diamonds."

"That is *so* not true." I laugh. "My only experience of diamonds is seeing them in shop windows."

"Then that must change," says Tom Rigbey. "Now, when can you lock your daughter in the cellar and have dinner with me?"

"What about tonight, Mum?" Freya suggests.

"Um. I'm not sure if—"

"Ninny'll babysit. You know she will. When does she ever say no?" To Tom, Freya says, "That's my gran. Our Wi-Fi's way faster than hers. She'd move in with us if she could."

Tom bows. "I greatly admire your strategic slant of mind, young lady. But we can't make plans unless your mother joins our little conspiracy. What shall we do to persuade her? I mean, it's only dinner. It's not as if we're proposing to blow up the Houses of Parliament."

Freya laughs and tucks her hair behind her ear. She's clearly delighted to be treated as if she's a key player. *Smart move, Talented Mr. Rigbey.*

"All right," I say. "Dinner tonight."

I'm glad this evening is still several hours away. So much has been said during this short conversation that I need to analyze. I want to make the arrangement as quickly as I can, so that I can get away from Tom Rigbey right now.

I need to get away from him so that I can think about him properly, without him there to distract me.

Chapter 7

WE MEET FOR dinner at eight o'clock, at a restaurant called the Oak Bistro, on Lensfield Place. I've never been here before, and it doesn't look like much from the outside, but inside it's beautiful: striking, colorful paintings with price tags attached occupying whole walls; thick white tablecloths and proper napkins—or, as Tom said when we sat down at our table, "None of your folded-paper nonsense." I notice there's an attractive outdoor eating area too, which must be fantastic in summer.

Will Tom and I ever sit out there? Will he still want to take me out for dinner by the time summer comes around?

Don't be an idiot, Chloe. Take it one day at a time.

I know why I'm feeling insecure, and I know how pathetic it is. Since we met this evening, Tom hasn't once mentioned marriage or diamonds. He seems to have two modes: frivolous and earnest. Tonight he's in earnest mode and not cracking silly jokes. He seems mainly to want to hear about my work and relationship history, and to tell me about his. Which is nice in a different way, but . . .

No. No buts. It's nice. I'm having a lovely time. It's just that after everything he said this afternoon, I was half expecting to arrive at the Oak Bistro and find him on one knee, holding out a diamond engagement ring, with a specially commissioned orchestra playing romantic music in the background.

I've read him wrong, clearly. He's not straightforwardly soppy and romantic. Thinking about it, he says some quite jarringly unromantic things. A straight-down-the-line romantic person wouldn't joke about stalking, murder and locking my daughter in the cellar.

Tom Rigbey is a highly unusual man. That doesn't mean he will never ask me to marry him. It's more likely to mean that, if he ever does, he will do it in a highly unusual way.

Not that I want to marry him, or would say yes. I barely know him.

I tell him about Freya's dad—my short relationship with him and our breakup. "That sounds tough," he says sympathetically. Then, with a more mischievous expression on his face, he says, "But your mother's been supportive, right? In exchange for great Wi-Fi?"

I laugh. "Actually . . . *now* she's great, and Freya's right—she'll babysit whenever I need her to, but that's only since she split up with Husband Number Three. When I was on my own with a six-month-old baby, Mum had only just met Clive and was pandering to his every need all day long. He was the child she looked after—and emotionally he was *such* a spoilt kid. She had no time for anyone else."

"Could you ever pander to a Clive?" Tom wrinkles his nose. "I couldn't. Names are important. I could pander to a Chloe, but never a Clive."

"What about your parents?" I ask him. I want to hear more details about his one and only serious relationship with a woman called Maddy, but he didn't have much to say about her, and moved on quite quickly once he'd told me they'd been together for four years, but split up when she'd moved to Australia for work. I'd feel intrusive if I revisited the subject.

I could ask about his parents instead. He hasn't mentioned them yet, and since we've just been discussing my mother . . . "You said you grew up in Manchester. Are your folks still there?"

"Did I say that?" He frowns. "When?"

"The first time we met. You mentioned the Palace Theater, where you saw *Joseph Dreamcoat*."

"There's going to be nothing left of that title by the time you finish with it, is there?" Tom chuckles. "Remind me if I ever need to fake my own death and invent a new ID, Joseph Dreamcoat's my name-in-waiting. You're quite right: I grew up in Manchester—and what an impressive memory you have! My brother Julian's still there. He has a dentistry practice there, in Fallowfield. My parents decamped to Fort Lauderdale, Florida, five years ago, in true retired-person style. I was sunbathing by their complex's shared swimming pool a few months ago and saw what I thought was the most enormous upright lizard—turned out to be an armadillo! I nearly freaked out, but managed to keep my cool for long enough to take a photo, which is now my Twitter avatar. Work weren't happy, but since I tweet purely in a personal capacity . . . and I did point out that the armadillo is far more handsome than I could ever hope to be. Okay, now I'm going to leave a gaping void in my chitchat so that you can say, 'Not at all, Tom—you are the sexiest man I've ever clapped eyes on.' "

I smile. I might have said something—nothing nearly so extreme as his suggestion, but something in that direction— had he not made it so awkward for me to do so.

Our main courses arrive—fishcakes for me and steak for Tom—and we carry on chatting. By the end of the meal I know that he is not interested in politics but plans to vote for Nick Clegg in the next election because "even though I have no clue what his policies are, he's been so savaged by the mob, I feel sorry for him." I learn, also, that Tom is fond of dogs (especially English bull terriers—as a child he had two, Butch and Sundance), a keen chess player and a cinema addict. His favorite old movie is *Whatever Happened to Baby Jane?*, the Joan Crawford and Bette Davis classic, and his favorite new one is *Prisoners*, starring Hugh Jackman and Jake Gyllenhaal. I've seen the first but not the second.

I don't have a favorite film, and say so when asked. "Then you'll need to get one, before the next time we meet," Tom says. "And please make sure it's not *Bridesmaids* or *Pretty Woman* or something hideous like that. Speaking of the next time we meet . . . I'd very much like to see you again. Are you free for dinner later in the week?"

"Who's Nadine Caspian?" I ask him. Shit. Why did I say

that? Why? I can't tell Tom what she said—he'd be shocked and hurt, and I'd be a bitch for passing on bad gossip that's probably has no justification whatsoever.

"Nadine?" He sounds and looks puzzled. "She's a receptionist at my firm."

"I know. I meant . . . is there anything between you and her?"

Tom's laugh suggests astonishment more than amusement. "Anything between me and Nadine? No. Not unless you mean the reception desk. I've said fewer than twenty words to her in my life."

"I'm sorry—it's none of my business. Forget I asked."

"Er, no. Why did you? Come on, what's going on? Why would ask me if there was anything between me and a receptionist I barely notice from one day to the next?"

"I think I must have imagined it: when I gave her the present and asked her to make sure you got it, she looked sort of . . . odd. I just wondered if she might be a secret admirer, if not a girlfriend or ex."

"Hm. I suppose it's possible she's a *very* secret admirer. She's never shown the remotest bit of interest in me. Now I come to think of it, she once showed no interest in getting a parcel I entrusted to her to its destination on time."

I feel a surge of excitement. This could be the explanation I'm looking for.

"Did you reprimand her for not sending the parcel?" A bollocking at work might be enough to make Nadine hate him.

Tom looks embarrassed. "Actually, funny you should ask that. No, I didn't. I hate socially awkward situations—I'm a real smoother-over by nature, hate conflict of any kind—so I pretended Nadine had done exactly the right thing by not sending the parcel. I made out I'd changed my mind and didn't want it to go out so soon after all, and silly old me for telling her it was urgent and needed to go straightaway."

"Oh." There goes my theory.

"So what about dinner later in the week? I mean, tomorrow's probably too soon, is it? Especially for your mum, newly stocked up on fiber-optic broadband as she is. Also—if I were you, I wouldn't want to see me again tomorrow. I'd be thoroughly sick of me by now. And, actually, I have to go to London first thing tomorrow, so maybe I'll need longer than a day to . . ." He breaks off and smiles enigmatically. "Sorry," he says. "Almost gave something away there. Oops—Tom the moron nearly strikes again."

"I'm not sick of you," I tell him.

Don't agree to tomorrow. Make him wait at least a few days.

Why? What's the point?

What did he nearly give away? The sooner I see him again, the sooner I'll find out.

"Tomorrow's fine for me if it works for you," I say.

Chapter 8

"I NEED TO speak to Nadine Caspian," I say to Rukia Yunis, the receptionist who conveyed my "Ash Grove" tiepin safely to Tom. Because she did this, I think of her as trustworthy. Perhaps that's crazy.

It's nine o'clock in the morning, the day after my dinner with Tom, also the day of my next dinner with Tom. I persuaded my mum to stay overnight. When she asked why I needed her to take Freya to school today, I mumbled something about an early garage appointment, then set off in my Volvo—the old, knackered one that Tom Rigbey missed his chance to steal—to CamEgo's offices.

Tom said he had to go to London first thing today, so it's the perfect opportunity. Now or never, I decided. I plumped for now. If Tom turns up at La Mimosa this evening with a beautiful diamond engagement ring and a marriage proposal—which of course he won't, but it's technically possible—I will need not to have a head full of doubts and fears planted by Nadine Caspian. I'd like to sort this out once and for all, so that I can stop thinking about it.

"Nadine?" says Rukia Yunis doubtfully.

"Yes. She's a receptionist here. You were sitting next to—"

"I know who she is. She . . . she doesn't work here anymore."

"What?"

"I'm as surprised as you are," Rukia says. "I've just this second opened the email announcement."

"What does it say? Did she resign? Wouldn't she give some notice?"

Rukia's eyes are fixed on the screen in front of her. She raises her eyebrows a little—not enough for me to be sure I'm not imagining it. Maybe her face hasn't moved at all. "I'm sorry, I can't share the contents of the email. But Nadine won't be in today, I'm afraid. Or . . ."

"Or ever?" I suggest.

"Right." Rukia nods. "Sorry. Is it anything I can help you with?"

I can't speak. Can't think of anything but Nadine's words: *I can't talk to you. If you're under his spell, you'll tell him anything I say. Tomorrow morning I'll find myself out of a job.*

Tom and I parted company at ten thirty last night. Would he have had enough time to get Nadine fired between then and this morning? I didn't tell him what she said about him, but did I say enough to make him see her as a potential threat?

"Can I ask you something?" I say to Rukia. "If Nadine's

gone, there's no reason why you shouldn't tell me: did you like her?"

"Like her?"

"Yes. Nadine. Did you trust her? Were the two of you friends?"

"Can't say I knew her particularly well. We got on okay, yeah. I trusted her as a colleague. I didn't confide in her or anything, but . . . I certainly had no reason not to trust her."

I ought to stop now. Leave.

"What about Tom Rigbey? Do you like and trust him?"

"Um . . ." Rukia laughs. "He's our CSO. It's not for the likes of me to have opinions about him."

"Don't be silly. There's no class system for opinions. Please be honest with me. I really need to know. Is Tom an okay guy, or is there something shady about him?"

"Shady?" Now she's giggling. "Tom Rigbey, shady? No, not at all. He can be a bit of a buffoon, but he's very sweet."

"A buffoon?"

"Yeah—certainly compared to most of the stuffed suits around here. He's also more interesting and entertaining than them. Tom's a character. Sometimes he walks along the corridor singing. He often forgets to take off his bicycle clips. Once he went into an important meeting with a smear of bike oil on his cheek. But everyone here likes him." Rukia leans toward me and lowers her voice. "Don't get me wrong: it helps that he's oh-my-God gorgeous and a science genius."

I exhale slowly. It's a relief to hear this. "Do you know why Nadine didn't like him?" I ask.

"I didn't know she didn't." Rukia looks surprised. "She never said anything to me."

No, because she didn't need to. Rukia wasn't in danger, as Nadine saw it.

"Please just tell me one thing: was Nadine fired?"

Rukia hesitates, then nods. "I don't know what for. Email doesn't say."

What could Nadine know about Tom that Rukia doesn't?

I don't believe he's dangerous. I don't. Even though Nadine was afraid she'd be fired and now she has been. It's just . . . if she wanted to put me off Tom because she was jealous, wouldn't she have said something more ordinary-sounding—"He'll use you for sex and then drop you"— something like that? Her choice of words makes it so much harder for me to disregard what she said. *Avoid him like the plague because that's what he is . . . Give him nothing, tell him nothing. . .*

That goes beyond any definition of normal bitchiness, surely.

Did Nadine give something to Tom Rigbey and suffer as a result? Did she tell him a secret and regret it?

My phone buzzes in my pocket twice. That means a text or email, not a phone call. It's not Lorna, then. Lorna would ring. I'm not answering her calls today, I've decided. She's too much of a mood wrecker.

I thank Rukia and leave. Outside on Hills Road, I pull out my phone. My heartbeat starts to gallop when I see it's a message from Tom. "Selfie outside New Bond Street Jeweler's Shop," it says. He's signed it "T xx." The attached photo is of

Tom standing in front of a window display of diamond rings, smiling his heart-stopping smile.

Oh, God. He's going to propose to me tonight. What else can this mean?

A sneery voice in my head—Lorna's? Nadine Caspian's?—says *This is the decisive moment, or it will be tonight at La Mimosa. You can't say you haven't been warned. Run, Chloe, run. Remember, you have to think of Freya's well-being too.*

I'm going to have to ring Lorna, even though the prospect of a grilling from her makes my throat close up. I can't think what else to do.

Chapter 9

"THIS IS SUCH a compelling case study," Lorna announces after a long silence. We're having lunch at the Green Man, in Trumpington. Well, she is. I'm staring at a tuna steak I have no desire to eat. "Can I say what strikes me immediately? You want to hear my analysis?"

I nod, though *want* is not quite the right word.

"Tom Rigbey is not keen on you in the normal sense of the word. He's not smitten in a good way—wanting to see you night after night, talking about diamond rings within milliseconds of making your acquaintance. Wait!" Lorna holds up a hand to stop me interrupting. "You can argue later. For now, just listen. Tom Rigbey is a stalker—a creepy latcher-on to strangers. Most women would run a mile from anyone who came on so scarily strong so quickly, but you didn't. Until I said *stalker*, you didn't think of him as one, did you?"

"No." I blink away tears. Maybe I'm naïve. Maybe falling for a charming, handsome, thoughtful science genius who is nicer to me than anyone else I've ever met is the height of stupidity. I'd be a better person, no doubt, if I accused strangers of being creepy, like Lorna does. "Tom isn't a stalker," I say.

"Yes, he totally is. You don't see it for a very simple reason: you're one too." Lorna smiles triumphantly. "Like I said: the two of you make for a compelling case study. I'm almost tempted to contact a psychology professor. Most victims of stalkers hate it and recognize the stalking for what it is. But imagine if a stalker happened to fixate on someone who's never had enough love or attention—maybe someone whose mother was a serial doormat for one husband after another, and who was always expected to take second place and fit in. This woman with the man-pleasing mother doesn't have such a great romantic history, by the way."

"I'd never have guessed," I murmur.

"She follows her mother's bad example and falls for the wrong guy: a chancer with avoidant personality disorder—undiagnosed—and before she knows what's hit her, he's scarpered, leaving her with a baby and a broken heart."

"Lorna?"

"What?"

"I'm not going to be any less offended because you're saying 'she' instead of 'you.' You don't need to talk about me in the third person."

"Offended? Don't be offended."

"Oh, okay then!"

"And don't be sarcastic either. You came to me because

you wanted to understand what's going on here, and you couldn't. I've worked it out. I'm helping you. Tom Rigbey, quite by chance, chose as his latest stalking victim someone so emotionally needy, she's incapable of recognizing stalking as stalking. You!" Lorna stares at me in obvious delight, as if I'm a rabbit she's just pulled out of a hat. "Wait! I know what you're going to say: you don't see yourself as emotionally needy because you're not clingy, pushy, harrassy in the way that most needy people are. On the contrary, you never ask for anything."

Lorna takes a break in her assassination of my character to sip her ginger beer shandy. She slurps in her eagerness to get going again, and spills a bit out of the side of her mouth.

"I've never thought about this before, but I reckon there are two types of needy," she goes on, wiping her chin. "Active and passive. Active is . . . Glenn Close's character in *Fatal Attraction*. She's the perfect example. Passive—or maybe covert's a better word, or humble—is you. All other things being equal, no one would ever know you were needy, least of all yourself, because you ask for nothing and expect nothing. You go through life accepting that you'll never be special, never be anyone's favorite person. Why should you be, right? Little old insignificant you? You neither hope nor expect to get your needs met, so, like a dutiful parent, you feed all your energy into caring for Freya. But then, boom! Out of the blue, Tom Rigbey comes along like a bolt of lightning . . . He's massively needy too, by the way, though he uses his wit and charm to conceal the void at his core. His good looks too—no one suspects how desperate he is because, come on, who wouldn't be supremely confident if they looked like that?"

Desperate. The word lodges at the center of my mind, in the bull's-eye spot.

Lorna's right. Who would think about marriage so early in a relationship unless they were desperate? Not even a relationship, come to think of it. An acquaintance. Why would a man of Tom Rigbey's caliber waste his time with me unless …

Unless he's so insecure that he'd fear abandonment if he went for a woman in the same league as him.

"Tom Rigbey, your knight in shining armor," Lorna warms to her theme. "He saves the day, gets Freya's music to the *Joseph* auditions in time to avoid disaster, lavishes flattery on both you and her, mentions diamonds and marriage terrifyingly quickly. At this point, any regular woman would think, 'Yikes, a stalker!' but not you—because, unknown to you, you've secretly always craved that kind of attention. To you he doesn't seem frighteningly single-minded and obsessive—he seems pleasingly attentive! Gratifyingly keen. I notice you're not denying it."

That's because I've temporarily lost the power of speech.

"You respond to his stalking by *stalking him back.*" Lorna couldn't be more delighted by her own cleverness. "You make him a tiepin with musical notes inside it from a song that's supposed to have some significance to the two of you—*way* over the top, as thank-you gifts go. You stay up half the night Googling him—"

"As did you," I point out.

"Only because I knew you were, and I suspected you'd make a hash of it. Then you take the present to his office when you could easily have posted it. Why didn't you? You were hoping to bump into him, that's why. And then you let him take you out for dinner, and another dinner the next night, despite being warned about him—"

"By a stranger!" I snap. "Would you take the word of a stranger—one who wasn't even prepared to be direct in her accusations—and avoid someone you liked, who had only ever been nice to you?"

Lorna pulls her face out of her pint glass and sighs. "Not nice, Chloe. Stalkerish. Please see sense. Look, think of it like this: imagine you meet a man who has this weird habit of constantly edging forward with his feet when he speaks to you. You'd find it annoying, wouldn't you? You're trying to talk to him but you can't concentrate because all the time he's shuffling closer and closer. Soon his face will be touching yours—eww! *Unless* . . . can you guess where I'm going with this?"

Outer Mongolia? I should be so lucky.

"Unless *you* have the equally weird habit of constantly edging *backwards* whenever you have a conversation, at exactly the same rate that he edges forwards. Then you wouldn't notice. You'd both be weirdos, but your weirdness would be camouflaged when you were together. See what I mean?"

"Unfortunately, yes."

Saying that I see doesn't stop Lorna from wanting to tell me again. "Both you and Tom Rigbey are predatory stalkers and grateful stalkees in equal measure. Hence, you're both able to maintain the illusion that you're just two normal people who are attracted to one another. Mystery solved!"

"Not the Nadine mystery," I say.

"Yes, Chloe! Ugh, get real. When Nadine described him as a plague and a danger, that must have been what she meant. Maybe he came on strong to her the way he is with you. She found his zealous persistence intimidating and told him to sod off. He then did something unspeakable to her as payback for the rejection—God knows what—and that's what she was hinting at. Chloe, Nadine was sacked *hours* after you mentioned her name to Tom in a she-might-be-jealous context. If that doesn't convince you, nothing will. He clearly panicked about what she might say to you if you met her again, and decided to get shot of her sharpish."

"You say 'clearly', but it's not clear. It's speculation."

"No, it's fact. Tom Rigbey is unhealthily obsessed with you. You don't see it because you're equally unhealthily obsessed with him. Something disastrous is almost definitely going to happen here! Men like that, who put you on a pedestal and call you ma'am . . . they're the ones who end up caving your skull in with a metal pipe when you burn their dinner and all their illusions about your perfection are shattered. Take my advice and heed Nadine's warning."

"No."

"Chloe, you don't know what he did to her! What would someone have to do to you to make you call them a plague in human form? Set fire to your house? Plant a bomb in your car?"

Lorna's words make my brain jolt. It's the strangest feeling: my mind does a full-circle turn and, at the end of it, everything looks different.

It's obvious what I must do.

"Chloe!" Lorna snaps her fingers in front of my face. "Did you hear what I just said?'

"Yes." Sort of. It was something about her knowing someone who could probably help me. "I don't need help."

Lorna sprays shandy across the table in her attempt not to laugh. "You forgot to add 'with my temporary insanity,' " she says. "Tough. You're getting the help whether you want it or not. They're only in Cambridge for a couple more days—it's too good an opportunity to miss. And . . ." She glances at her watch. "At the risk of pissing you off still further, I've made the arrangement already. We'd better get a move on—we're meeting them in twenty minutes."

"Who?" I ask.

Lorna rolls her eyes. "I knew you weren't listening," she says.

Chapter 10

"THEY" TURN OUT to be Lorna's old schoolfriend Charlotte and her husband, Simon. We've met them in the Eagle. Both are police officers—he's some kind of hotshot murder detective and she's more in the social-work sphere of policing: community crime forums, suicide prevention initiatives, that kind of thing.

I don't want to be here, but I can't deny I'm finding them interesting so far. I'm enjoying wondering about them. She, Charlotte, seems to flinch every time Lorna speaks, which makes me warm to her.

Her husband has hardly said a word, and keeps directing the fiercest of evil stares at anyone nearby who laughs or clinks their glass too loudly, but he earned my admiration on arrival by asking if we could move to a quieter part of the pub. Thanks to him, we're sitting in the room I always want to sit in and am normally not allowed to by Lorna because it's not historical enough—the one to the right of the front door.

Why is he so resentful of normal pub noise? It's odd. Also strange is their reason for being in Cambridge. Apparently Charlotte's sister is staying at the Varsity Hotel for a week with her boyfriend. That was the explanation offered, with no extra detail provided, apart from, "We're here to keep an eye on them." Perhaps that was a joke and the four are all on holiday together, but that wasn't my impression. Charlotte made it sound more as if she and Simon were spying on her sister and the boyfriend.

I feel guilty for taking up any of their time, and pathetic for allowing Lorna to bring me here and subject me to this. I close my eyes and try to magic myself out of the room while she tells the story so far in her own special way. Once she's finished, Charlotte says, "Chloe? You haven't said anything. Do you disagree with Lorna?"

I don't know what to say. I'm sure of my answer, but I feel no need to share my opinion of the matter with anyone. It would be rude to say nothing, though, and I don't want to be rude to anyone who prefers me to Lorna, as Charlotte seems to.

"There's no proof of anything," I say. "Maybe Tom's dangerous, but maybe Nadine Caspian was mistaken. Or just plain lying for some reason. I don't know. I have higher standards of evidence than Lorna."

She can't let that go unchallenged. "There's no proof, but there's plenty of circumstantial evidence," she says. "More than enough for a guilty verdict, in my view." So now she's making a court case out of it: I'm the defense to her prosecution. Poor judges. I bet they wish they'd never agreed to meet us.

"Chloe's right that what Nadine says is hearsay only," says Charlotte.

Thank you.

"Nadine got fired," Simon says. "She was worried she'd get fired if she spoke up, and she did. I agree with Lorna that her use of extreme language—the plague stuff—makes a real threat more likely. Not only because of the language itself, but because of what went before it."

"What do you mean?" I ask him.

"The conversation you and Nadine had before you mentioned Tom Rigbey's name, assuming Lorna described it accurately—there were no unusual turns of phrase. The opposite, in fact. She spoke in clichés: 'have a nosey', 'the man in your life', 'a prezzie for me, and it's not even my birthday'. Then when you mentioned Rigbey, her vocabulary became more distinctive: 'give him nothing, tell him nothing, trust him not at all.' That's pretty memorable—some might say poetic. 'A plague in human form'—also strong and attention-grabbing. It's not evidence of anything, but if I had to guess, I'd say a sudden burst of fear or anger, provoked by hearing Rigbey's name when she didn't expect to, caused her to switch from clichéd conversational coasting-along to vivid authentic expression."

I nod and try to look as if I appreciate this insight.

"On the other hand . . ." Simon scratches his badly shaved chin. "I don't know. From what you've told us, Rigbey's handsome, confident, successful. Probably more dazzlingly brilliant than his colleagues. Put someone like that in a workplace and you'll see a breakout of Tall Poppy syndrome—people will set out to mow him down."

"Not the admin staff, surely?" Charlotte says. "Is it likely that Nadine the receptionist would be jealous of the CSO? I reckon she's more likely to envy a better-paid receptionist."

"Woman scorned," Simon mutters. "That's the simplest explanation, if she's lying about Rigbey. Which means it's unlikely to be that."

"It's unlikely to be the simplest explanation?" I say, wondering if I've misheard.

Simon nods. "Nothing is simple. The true explanation for anything you don't understand is likely to be so complex, you'll never fully grasp it."

"How comforting," says Lorna sarcastically. "I disagree. The simplest explanation is that Tom Rigbey's dangerous and best avoided. Anyone who can't fully grasp that is mentally challenged. He butted into Chloe's conversation with Freya and demanded that she hand over her car keys. He sucked up to Freya, calling her 'Your Highness,' deliberately ingratiating himself with her to win Chloe over. Then, in response to Chloe's present, he *stakes out* Freya's rehearsal, knowing Chloe will be there, and in their next conversation—only the second they've ever had— he mentions marriage and hints at diamond engagement rings. As if that's not enough, he jokingly refers to imprisoning Freya in a cellar."

"It was a joke," I say to myself more than anyone else.

"Yeah, one that tells us a lot about him." Lorna's eyes

flare with anger. "His idea of humor is interesting. It seems to consist of . . . lying, basically. 'Where did you get the tiepin from? Oh, I know: the Folk Song Tiepins Warehouse just off the M11.' We all know no such place exists! I know you'll say that was also only a joke, Chloe, but the fact is, Tom Rigbey habitually peppers his small talk with bullshit. So, it's likely he does the same with his . . ." Lorna stops, searching for the right word.

"With his big talk?" I suggest.

"Yes. Every tiny detail—everything!—points in the direction of him being untrustworthy and unsafe. What about the 'If I ever fake my own death' joke? And calling himself the 'Talented Mr. Rigbey'—that's a reference to the Talented Mr. Ripley, a charming and devious fictional *murderer*. A psychopath."

"That might be stretching a point," says Simon. "His name's Tom. Mr. Ripley's name: also Tom. The similarity would occur to most people, I think. If my name were Tom Rigbey, I'm sure I'd make that joke more than once in my life."

"You wouldn't," Charlotte tells him. "I'd have to make it for you, and you'd get cross with me."

"What about him saying that Chloe had better not choose *Bridesmaids* or *Pretty Woman* as her favorite film? You don't think that's sinister control-freaky at all, telling her what movies are acceptable? And look at his self-confessed favorites: *Whatever Happened to Baby Jane?*—about twisted people who aren't what they first appear to be—and *Prisoners*, which sails close to the wind in condoning torture."

"My favorite movies are *Jaws* and *An Officer and a Gentleman*," says Charlotte. 'I'm neither a naval aviator nor a shark."

"Every single word out of his mouth is just . . . *off*," says Lorna wearily. I remind myself that she has never heard any of his words—only what I've relayed back to her. "How can you not see it, Chloe? What about when he reveled in the fact that lyrics of *Joseph* are so terrible? You told me he said, 'It's just *awful*,' gleefully, as if he enjoyed awful things most of all."

"But you could do that with anyone's speech!" I snap. "Twist it, analyze it so closely that—"

"There's no point in any of this," Simon cuts in abruptly. "We're going back and forth, getting nowhere. Chloe, would you like us to check this guy out, put your mind at rest?"

"Yes, she would," says Lorna.

"Chloe?" Charlotte asks pointedly. I'm grateful to her for noticing that I'm a person with a mind of my own, not a ventriloquist's dummy.

I'm torn. Yes, I want to know, especially if there's something about Tom that he'll never tell me. I want to know every single thing about him, the best and the worst, but if I say that, I'll be misunderstood.

I have to take the risk. I can't pass up this chance. "Are you allowed to . . . check people out, when they've committed no crime?" I ask.

"No," says Charlotte. "So don't tell anyone we did, okay?"

"It depends," says Simon, as if the question hasn't just been answered. "If there's possible danger involved, it's a different story."

"What we're allowed to do and what's the right thing to do aren't always the same thing," Charlotte tells me.

"My hunch is that if we look, we'll find something of interest," says Simon. "I don't like threats that linger unnoticed. They tend to grow and keep growing. Plus, I'm curious. I'd send you to Cambridge police, but they'll be by-the-book about it, so . . . tell me everything you know about Tom Rigbey and I'll get on it. In the meantime, stay away from him."

I can't do that—I'm having dinner with Tom tonight—but I'm happy to share everything I know about him with Simon. It's not much.

"He grew up in Manchester," I say. "His parents now live in Fort Lauderdale, Florida. They moved there five years ago. He has a brother who's a dentist in Fallowfield in Manchester—Julian—and a friend called Keiran who's got a very expensive BMW sports car—a hundred grand, Tom said. Some people broke into it recently and left it full of burger wrappers and cider bottles. He's had one serious relationship with a woman called Maddy. They were together four years, but then she moved to Australia for work."

"Girlfriend escapes down under, parents flee to Florida," Lorna mutters. "Sounds to me like everyone can't wait to get away from the Talented Mr Rigbey."

"Anything else, Chloe?" Charlotte asks. "Literally, anything at all might be useful, however daft it seems."

"Um . . . he told me his Twitter avatar is a photo of an armadillo he saw next to his parents' pool in Florida. He used to have two English bull terriers as pets: Butch and Sundance."

"Butch and Sundance?" Lorna pounces. "You never told me that!" She turns to Simon. "Could this *be* any more obvious? Butch Cassidy and the Sundance Kid—two outlaws!"

"Or, if we want to be reasonable about this . . ." says Charlotte, who seems to like contradicting Lorna, and is braver about it than I am, " . . . English bull terriers are a butch-looking breed of dog. Aren't they the ones with the enormous protruding faces that look as if they're made of rock? If I had a dog like that, the name Butch might well spring to mind."

"Sundance," I say. "Dancing merrily in the sun. Must mean Tom's a happy person who loves dancing."

Charlotte laughs appreciatively.

"Leave it with us, Chloe," says Simon. "Let's meet here again the day after tomorrow."

Chapter 11

I STAND APART from the other parents in the school play-ground as we wait for the end-of-day bell to ring, and use my phone to search the Internet for references to Nadine Caspian.

I can't wait two days for more information. I have to do something right now. Every nerve in my body is buzzing with a need to act. I might not be a police detective, but I care more than Simon and Charlotte do. And they aren't the only ones who can check things out.

If I can find Nadine's address, I'm going to pay her a visit. She can't say what she said to me, then change her mind and disappear. It's not fair.

Her name is unusual. That should make it easier to find her. There can't be many Nadine Caspians in Cambridge.

First I'll force it out of her: what she knows, what she thinks will make me turn my back on Tom. I want to tell her that nothing will. Nothing ever could.

This is the realization that jolted my brain while Lorna was harassing me earlier: I've been sick with fear since Nadine said what she said on the stairs at CamEgo, but I shouldn't have been. I only need to worry if it would make a difference—if there *is* something, anything, I could learn about Tom that would change the way I feel.

If my love for Tom were conditional upon him being a good, harmless person, then I would right now be at the mercy of Nadine, Simon, Charlotte, Lorna. Any of them, at any time, could present me with a previously unknown fact about him that would ruin everything.

I realized earlier that the opposite is true.

Nothing could put me off Tom. Whatever he's done, whatever he is, I love him and will always love him. I can't help it. There's no point pretending that any moral principle could make the blindest bit of difference. I've never felt this way about anyone before. Since our first meeting, there has been no room in my head for anything but Tom Rigbey. I've been floating on the happiness that his existence and interest in me has brought into my life. If he's bombed a car or set fire to a house, I don't care. If he's killed someone, or tried to and failed, I don't care. If every word out of his mouth is a calculating lie, so what? No one else has ever made me feel as elated as I feel in his presence—not even for ten minutes.

Not at all.

So. I have to not care. It's the only way I can be immune to what Simon and Charlotte might be about to find out and tell me.

If Tom is a plague in human form, and I'm ready to condone all of his sins, then I must be one too.

I should do something wrong, to prove that we belong together, that we're right for each other. Something Nadine Caspian can find out about and say, "Ugh, Chloe Daniels is every bit as bad as Tom Rigbey. They deserve each other."

Maybe I could do something wrong *to* Nadine Caspian. Now there's an idea . . .

The school bell rings, startling me, at the exact same moment that I find Nadine on Twitter. There's her horrible face as her avatar, smiling. Like a doll made of flesh-colored stone. I have a quick look up and down her timeline. Her communications are mostly inane: clothes, booze, cake baking. A new tweet appears, moving the others down on my phone's screen. She must have just done it. It's a quote. It says, " 'Pour yourself a drink put on some lipstick and pull yourself together'— Elizabeth Taylor." There should be comma after *drink*.

I press the "Reply" icon at the bottom of Nadine's latest offering, and write, "Why are you so against Tom Rigbey? What's he ever done to you?" Then I press the "tweet" button.

Her reply appears on her timeline a few minutes later. "He's a sociopath. Leave me alone. Blocking you now."

A sociopath? The word is like cold medicine, making me swallow hard. What does it even mean?

I'll look it up later. If Tom Rigbey is a sociopath, then I must become one too. *Oh, God.* I hold my breath and clench my fists, nearly knocked off balance by sudden weakness. I'm not sure I can do this. *Please let this whole thing be one enormous misunderstanding.*

"Mum!" Freya calls out, running toward me. "I won the Star of the Week award!"

"That's wonderful, darling. Well done." I say all this without registering what she's told me. I'm too lost in my own thoughts.

If I find out the truth about Tom and say nothing, he'll think I don't know.

The possibility that I know and don't mind because I love him unconditionally will not occur to him.

Chapter 12

"Do you hate it? Tell me if you hate it, and I'll ... scoot over and propose to that woman over there instead. No, I'm kidding. Is it okay?"

I stare tearfully at the large pear-shaped diamond in its open, cushioned box. "It's beautiful," I manage to say. "Stunning." Any minute now, the La Mimosa staff will spot the ring and this will no longer be a private conversation.

I won't be able to say no, surrounded by Italian waiters.

I don't want to say no. There's a big, loud "YES" in my head.

Tom looks delighted. "Try it on, see if it fits. If it doesn't, I can get it altered. No, wait! Don't try it on."

"Why not?'

"I think you need to accept first—officially. You need to say you want to marry me. Assuming you do. If you don't, that's fine. I'll just wade into the River Cam with my pockets full of heavy stones. That's why I picked this restaurant—the river's right outside, full of the bodies of spurned suitors." He grins. He knows I'm going to say yes.

Am I, though? If I am, what's stopping me? Not his over-the-top, macabre sense of humor. I like that about him. Other people's chatter has started to seem duller since I met Tom. Every sentence he utters contains a big surprise. Listening to him, talking to him, is the conversational equivalent of unwrapping presents all the time.

What's stopping me accepting Tom's proposal is that I'm not being honest with him. If he knew the truth, he might realize he doesn't love me that much after all. How would he feel if I told him that, earlier today, I asked two police officers to look into his background for me? I could explain that I'd only done it in the hope of exonerating him, but would that soften the blow?

Tom's love for me might not be as unconditional as mine for him. I can't take the risk. It's not only that I'm certain he'd be furious if he knew I'd asked two strangers to spy on him. There's something else too. What if, psychologically, he needs to pretend that the mistakes of the past never happened in order to survive in the present? What if part of my attraction for him is that I don't know about the terrible things he did, assuming they're real?

If I were to say to him, "I know you're a sociopath, and it doesn't make me love you any less," that might not make him happy. It might ruin everything, if it matters to him to remain in denial.

"Chloe? You look worried. Is everything okay?" Tom puts

his head in his hands. 'I'm such an idiot," he says. "You're an *idiot*, Rigbey! Proposing out of the blue to a woman who barely knows you—"

"No, it's not that," I try to say, but he talks over me.

"Look, Chloe, I know it's too soon to be thrusting diamond rings in your face. I've just dived straight in, like a reckless kid—I knew it was a risky strategy, but the thing is . . . I spent four years with Maddy, living with her, never sure of whether to propose or not because I just didn't know. I felt as if I ought to want to marry her—sometimes I was almost convinced I did—but it also seemed possible that, in fact, I didn't. That living together was enough. It wasn't enough for her, though, and when she left for Australia, although I missed her, I wasn't a wreck. I wasn't distraught. I could envisage a life without her. I assumed I was just a moderate sort of person who might never marry anybody—which I thought would be fine, because my work's so all-consuming. I thought work was my passion in life." He stops. Frowns.

"And?" I prompt him.

"And then I saw you on Bridge Street and . . . well, actually it wasn't only love at first sight. I heard your voice, too. Her Highness might be the singer of the family, but . . . you have a lovely voice, Chloe. Even when you're yelling like a Wall Street trader whose entire collection of shares has just . . . deflated, or whatever shares do. I fell in love with you, and I thought to myself, 'That's the woman I'm going to marry. That disheveled shouty one over there.'"

"Tom—stop."

"Ah. Okay. Oh dear." He looks dejected.

"I want to say yes, I really do—"

"You do?" He perks up. "Excellent! Then say it."

"Tom, there are . . . things about me that you don't know. Things you might not like if you knew."

"Such as?"

I hear Nadine Caspian's voice in my head: *Tell him nothing, trust him not at all.*

"There are things you don't know about me," Tom says cheerfully. "When I was in my early twenties, I pretended I was allergic to fish. Not just mildly. I led all my colleagues to believe—well, I *told* them—that if I consumed so much as a drop of fish oil, I'd very likely die."

I laugh. "Er . . . why?"

"Long story. The simple explanation being youthful foolishness. Basically, I went out drinking one night with friends when I should have been getting an early night before an important work away-day. Next morning I found myself temporarily paralyzed and incapable of anything more demanding than puking into a bucket. I was too sick to stagger to the bathroom. If I'd told my boss the truth, he'd have thought, rightly, that he ought to promote someone else—someone less hedonistic and more responsible. I considered offering a lame excuse like food poisoning, but no one would have believed it, so in a moment of desperate panic, I trotted out a story that no one would think to doubt because it was so . . . extreme. And tragic, too. Poor me: ever-present risk of ghastly early haddock death, what a great loss, et cetera."

"But . . . in the story, how did you explain why you'd eaten fish if you were so allergic?" If I'd been Tom's girlfriend in those days, I could have helped him to eliminate continuity errors from the lies he told his boss.

"A very astute question." Tom chuckles. "As I recall, my story involved a curry house kitchen being culpably negligent and allowing a sliver of cod to fall into my kofta Madras. Everyone at work was enormously sympathetic, as per my cunning plan. I got the promotion, and was stuck with a fake allergy. Remembering the lie and acting accordingly was so exhausting, I left within a year and started a new life at a different firm, where I quickly established my bona fides as an enthusiastic fish eater."

"I've never seen you eat fish," I tell him, looking at the chicken liver pate and melba toast on his plate. "You've ordered meat whenever I've had meals with you. Not even a prawn cocktail starter."

"Wait—you're accusing me of lying about *not* having a fish allergy?" Tom teases me.

"Do you think anyone can ever really trust anyone?" I ask him.

"Yes. I trust you," he says. "Now, since you've heard mine, please spill all your guilty secrets. I promise you, I'm a hundred percent unputoffable."

Yes, because he's a stalker. Lorna's voice this time.

I wish they'd shut up, all these more-sensible-people-than-me who have somehow managed to invade my mind. I need to be able to hear my own thoughts, draw my own conclusions.

"Or, if you'd prefer, you can remain mysterious," Tom suggests. "I like a good mystery. If you want to keep quiet about your shady past as a drug kingpin, that's fine by me. What is a kingpin, by the way? I'm not sure I've ever known."

I love him. And I've never heard the word *shady* said in such a wholesome way.

"Yes," I say.

"Yes what? Oh!" Tom's eyes widen. "You mean . . . *yes, yes?*"

"Yes. Yes yes."

"You'll marry me?"

"Haven't you had enough yeses yet?" I take the diamond ring from the box and slide it onto my finger. "It's a bit loose. Sorry."

"Damn. I'd better order you another pizza, with extra cheese—fatten you up." Suddenly Tom looks worried. "Do you want to check with Freya before saying yes-yes?"

"No. If she complains, I'll put her up for adoption." I laugh. Tom doesn't.

Sorry. Just a little sociopath joke there.

I think of *West Side Story*, the musical my school put on when I was seventeen. Tom is right: I do have a nice voice. Long before Freya was born, I was the singer of the family. As Maria in *West Side Story*, I sang, "I love him. I'm his. And everything he is, I am too." I sing those words again now, in my head.

"I think it should be fine?" Tom says as if he's asking a question. "Freya likes me, doesn't she? Damn, maybe the forgotten-music emergency dash wasn't enough. I might have to buy a God costume, appear in her room in the middle of the night and say in a deep booming voice that I decree Tom

Rigbey must marry her mother and nothing must stand in his way."

"Oh, I thought you were already wearing your God costume," I say drily. 'I assumed you had it on permanent loan."

For the first time since we met, Tom laughs at my joke as much as I laugh at all of his.

Chapter 13

THE NEXT DAY, Lorna and I meet Simon and Charlotte again—not at the Eagle this time, but, bizarrely, at the market's waffle stall in the square. Simon's choice, according to Lorna, because he didn't like the Eagle yesterday. Apparently neither Charlotte nor Lorna succeeded in suggesting another indoor venue that met with his approval.

What the hell's wrong with him? Why didn't he like the Eagle? How can an open-to-the-elements market stall be the best option? It's cold, windy, raining, and the four of us are shivering in plastic chairs around a wobbly table. Our heads are protected from the rain by a canvas cover, but we're still getting damp because it's blowing in horizontally. Simon didn't even order a waffle—just a cup of tea. The man who handed it to him, who is now making waffles for the rest of us, keeps shooting bemused looks in our direction. I can tell he's thinking, "Why on earth do they want to sit here on a day like today?"

One good thing about being freezing cold is that I can keep my scarf wrapped tightly around my neck and hide the gold chain I don't normally wear. My engagement ring is dangling from the end of it, since it's currently too loose to wear on my finger, and Lorna would spot it straightaway, given half a chance.

Everyone assumed I would cancel my dinner with Tom last night. No one has thought it worth asking me today, to check that I did.

Simon's holding a notebook in his hand—the kind only a man would choose, with nothing decorative about it. He's not reading from its pages yet, but he stares at it as he speaks, as if his dialogue is written down there. "All right, there's a lot of detail and none of it remarkable, so you'll need to pay attention. I'll repeat it if I have to but I'd rather not have to."

I'd rather not be accused in advance of falling short when I've done nothing wrong, but, unlike Simon, I'm too polite to say so.

"Overview first, then specifics," he says in the same slightly disapproving tone. "Everything Tom Rigbey told you about himself and his life appears to be true. He's got no criminal record. On paper he seems to be a blameless citizen."

I'm basking in the warmth of the relief that's flooding my system when Simon adds, "That's why I said listen carefully. You'll also need to *think* carefully. The answer—the missing information—isn't obvious, but it's here, contained in what you already know and what I'm about to tell you. Once you see it, you can't miss it . . . but you might have to look hard in order to see it."

Charlotte says, "I feel obliged to say, Chloe: I haven't a clue what Simon's talking about, and I've heard the full spiel twice already today, so you're not the only one in the dark."

I don't understand. Isn't she his wife? Why didn't she ask him to explain it to her before they got here? That's what I would have done.

"Tom Rigbey was born in Levenshulme, Manchester, in 1981. He has one brother—Julian, the Fallowfield dentist—and a sister, Rebecca. Did he mention her to you?"

"Yes, but not by name. He said they weren't close."

"They aren't," Simon agrees. "She lives in London and works for the CBI."

"Which is what?" I ask.

"The Confederation of British Industry."

"Oh." I'm none the wiser. Okay. Tom's sister works . . . somewhere businessy. That'll do. "He told me she lived in London."

"Right. Parents—Fort Lauderdale, Florida, for the last five years, as he said. They have a shared swimming pool at their apartment building, as Tom described, and I've found no reason to disbelieve that the armadillo in his Twitter avatar isn't one he encountered and photographed beside that pool."

"Is the armadillo relevant to anything?" Lorna asks impatiently.

"Anything might be relevant," says Charlotte. "We don't know yet."

"No," Simon says flatly. "The armadillo's got fuck all to do it. Forget him. It," Simon corrects himself.

"Right." Charlotte mutters. She looks disappointed. We sit in silence for a while. I suspect I'm not the only one disobediently remembering the armadillo.

"Tom's friend Keiran with the expensive BMW—that's also true." Simon plows on. "Keiran Connaughton. He and Tom were in the same year at Manchester Grammar School and have stayed friends since. Bear in mind, one sign that someone's a dangerous sociopath is if they have no one in their life who dates back very far—no one in a position to reveal that they've changed their various stories over the years. But . . . not the case here."

There's that word again: *sociopath*.

And if it's not the case that Tom has no long-standing friendships, if he's not a sociopath, then what bad and dangerous kind of person is he? What's the problem? Simon's tone strongly suggests there is one and that it's serious, but I can't work out what I'm supposed to be listening for.

"The burger-wrappers-and-empty-cider-bottles-in-expensive-sports-car story? Completely true," he says. "I've seen no evidence that Tom is dishonest. Butch and Sundance, the bull terriers? True."

"You contacted Keiran?" I say, surprised.

"Charlie spoke to him."

"Charlie?"

"Me," says Charlotte. "Everyone calls me Charlie except Lorna, who refuses to."

"Because it's a cheap-and-nasty perfume, a life-destroying drug, and horribly unisex," Lorna explains.

"Can we not get sidetracked?" says Simon. "Maddy, the

ex-girlfriend, is in Australia where she's supposed to be. She had only good things to say about Tom. So, let's move on to his education and work history. After Manchester Grammar School for boys, he was an undergraduate and then a graduate at Peterhouse, here. He got the best results in his year when he graduated, and he's worked for three companies since. He started his career at Sagentia, just outside Cambridge. Got promoted through the ranks very quickly there. Then he went to Intel, who we've all heard of, and worked there for a few years, in America."

I've heard of Intel but I can't say I'm sure what it is. A computer company? Tom has never told me he lived and worked in America. My stomach tenses. Is it coming now, the shocking revelation?

"He got promoted by Intel, stayed there for four years, then made another move: back to England, to CamEgo. He's been promoted twice since he got there, and now holds the top position that someone in his field can: CSO."

Finally, Simon looks up, in time to see three waffles with toffee sauce and maple syrup heading toward our table. "That's it," he says. "That's everything I found out."

Chapter 14

THE SUGAR RUSH from my waffle—which is probably delicious, but I barely taste it—ought to make my brain move faster, but it's not working. Neither is the caffeine from my second cup of tea. "I don't get it," I tell Simon. "I listened as carefully as I've ever listened to anything—I don't need you to repeat a single word—but I didn't hear anything worrying or suspicious."

"Me neither," says Charlie.

Simon jerks his head at Lorna. "What about you?"

She'll never admit she spotted nothing. Never. After a few seconds, she says, "His three jobs—did he move around by choice from company to company, or was he sacked? You say he 'went' from Sagentia to Intel, then 'made another move' to CamEgo . . ."

Simon lurches forward, nearly knocking over our flimsy plastic table. "That's the question I was hoping to hear." He looks happy, or what I assume is happy for him. Not grumpy, anyway.

"I think it's a daft question," I say. "Sorry, Lorna, but . . . Intel, CamEgo—these are serious companies. He wouldn't have got a job at either without amazing references from his previous employers, would he? And he wouldn't have got those if he'd been fired."

"Are you sure?" Simon asks me.

My breath catches in my throat. "No, but—"

"Forget guessing and focus on what we know. Facts. Indisputable ones. When were you planning to tell me you tweeted Nadine Caspian yesterday?"

"You did *what*?" says Lorna.

"Do you want me to find out the truth for you or not?" Simon glares at me. "If you do, tell me everything."

"Simon!" Charlie hits his arm with her toffee-sauce-stained plastic fork. "Chloe isn't a criminal. She doesn't have to tell you a single iota more than she wants to."

"I didn't mention it only because I thought it was neither here nor there," I say, feeling my face heat up.

"Yeah, well, luckily I found it, and it points in the same direction as everything else. Your tweet to Nadine: 'What have you got against Tom Rigbey?' or words to that effect. Hers to you: 'He's a sociopath. Leave me alone. You're blocked.' You didn't find that interesting?"

"No." I blink away tears. "I found it nasty and slanderous and . . ."

"Slanderous?" Simon leaps on the word. "Because she didn't back it up with facts?"

"No, she didn't."

"She gave you only one word to go on: sociopath. Still, it's a big one, as words go. Has Tom said anything to you about being fired? Sorry, I'll rephrase that: has he ever mentioned the circumstances in which he left either Sagentia or Intel?"

"No! I've hardly had a chance to speak to him about anything. We've only just met."

And yet you're wearing a diamond ring—a ring that means you intend to marry him—on a chain around your neck.

I don't know why I do what I do next. It's an urge I can't restrain. Perhaps I'm impatient to have the worst over with. I remove my scarf, hook my finger around the gold chain and pull it out so that the ring is visible. "I had dinner with Tom last night," I say. "We're engaged."

"Jesus frigging Christ on an arsehole cracker!" Lorna declares.

"Aren't you training to be some kind of cleric?" Charlie asks her.

"Good," says Simon.

"*Good*?" I repeat, baffled.

"Yeah. It was the next thing I was going to urge you to do: stop avoiding him, and behave toward him exactly as you would if you weren't suspicious. I was going to say: if he proposes, which you seemed to think he might, say yes. Might seem like odd advice, but you'll understand in due course." Simon shrugs. "You've already seen him and agreed to marry him, though, so. No need for me to steer things in that direction."

"Urgh!" Charlie groans. "Simon—sorry about this,

Chloe—just *tell* her, and tell us all while you're at it. Why can't we understand right now instead of in due course?"

"Yes, especially if you're planning to use Chloe as some sort of bait," Lorna agrees. "She needs to know what level of risk she's dealing with. How dangerous is Tom Rigbey?"

"Simon." Charlie waves her hand in front of his face. He appears to have drifted into a trance-like state. "If you've found out that Tom was sacked from one or both of his previous jobs, tell us. Why was he fired?"

Simon fixes his eyes on me: an intense stare. "I assume you looked up a definition of sociopathy, after reading Nadine's tweet?"

I nod.

"So you know that a key trait of sociopaths is the inability to hold down a job or stay in one place for very long?"

"Tom's been at CamEgo for long enough to be promoted several times," I say. "Talented, ambitious people often change jobs."

"So do sociopaths with forged references," says Simon. "Who ever checks that references are from the person they're meant to be from?"

"Simon, stop tormenting her," murmurs Charlie. "Whatever you've found out, whatever you know . . . seriously. Out with it."

"Not found out," he says. "Worked out. You really can't see it? None of you?"

"No, we can't," Lorna speaks for all of us. "I did pretty well guessing Tom had been fired, but there's a limit to how much we can guess."

"Apparently," says Simon bitterly. This is unbelievable. He's angry with us for not being mind readers.

"So Tom got fired. So what?" I say. "I don't care. Who hasn't been fired at some point or another?" I haven't, but that's beside the point. I can pretend I have if necessary. If that's what I have to do to stand by Tom, I'll do it. "Did he get fired for pretending to have a food allergy?"

"What the ever-loving fuck?" Lorna whirls around to face me. "Where did that come from?'

"No. What makes you say that?" Simon asks me.

"Nothing. Forget it."

"Come on." Abruptly, Simon stands up. "No, not all of you. Just Chloe. We're going to see Nadine Caspian. You need to hear her story. Until you do, you won't understand. It's not going to be easy for her to tell it, or for you to believe it, but it's the only way."

Chapter 15

HALF AN HOUR later, Simon and I are outside Nadine Caspian's house: a beige newly constructed three-story that some might call a terrace and some a maisonette.

"Ready?" says Simon.

I nod. Yes, I'm ready, but for what?

He rings the bell, then stands and stares at it, as if expecting it to reply to him directly.

I'm wearing my engagement ring on my wedding finger because he told me to. I didn't want to without knowing why, but I did it. I don't want to have to see or speak to Nadine Caspian, but here I am: bribed by the promise that soon I will know everything.

Without warning, tears fill my eyes—tears that have to be gone by the time Nadine opens the door or Simon turns to look at me, whichever happens first. I blink frantically. Squeeze my eyes shut. *Better.*

I hate this. Not only the doubt surrounding Tom, but also I hate that this used to be my thing to wonder about—my problem, mine alone—and I seem to have handed over control to . . . well, to everybody. I'm not in charge of anything, least of all myself, and I want to be. If I were braver I'd take Freya and disappear to somewhere far away from Lorna, Simon the peculiar policeman, Nadine Caspian . . . I don't want any of these people in my life, so why are they?

Don't be silly—Lorna's your best friend.

And Tom? Do you want him in your life?

Yes, I do. Whoever he is, whatever he's done, I want him. I love him. I'm also frightened that loving him might be about to get harder. So far, I've been able to present a defense based on my belief in his innocence, but what if that's about to change? What if he did something truly terrible, and there are no mitigating circumstances, and I don't stop loving him? I'm worried that, if that happens, I won't be able to defend myself.

"Come on," Simon breathes, pressing the bell again.

"She might be out," I say, and he looks affronted.

My phone buzzes in my pocket. I pull it out and look at the screen. "It's a text from Tom," I say.

"Show me."

Of course: my fiancé might be a dangerous sociopath, so from now on I must hand over all private messages to the police.

I pass my phone to Simon. Tom has sent a photo of himself sitting at a table—it looks as if it might be the CamEgo staff canteen—with a salmon fillet on a plate in front of him. His message says, "See? No fish allergy! T xx"

"Text back as if nothing's wrong," says Simon. I flinch at what this must mean. "It's some kind of joke, so be jokey in your response. Send kisses back—whatever you'd normally do. You're his trusting fiancée as far as he's concerned, so act like it."

Nothing is wrong. Nothing is wrong.

I start to compose a message to Tom: "Fish on plate, not in mouth—not proof of eating! Pictures or it didn't happen, as my friend Lorna would say. C xx"

"Wait—she's coming." Simon moves closer to the door. "I heard something moving inside." He presses the bell a third time. "Let me see that before you send it."

Too numb to do anything but obey, I show him my reply.

"Good. That's good." He smiles, not entirely successfully. As if he hasn't had much practice. His mouth looks like a Venetian blind that's been hiked up too much on one side.

A serious crime must be involved, or he wouldn't be here. He wouldn't care enough to give up his time.

The door in front of us opens, and I'm face-to-face with Nadine again. She's wearing black tracksuit bottoms and a pink cotton hoodie. Her eyes widen. "How did you . . . ?" She gawps at me.

"How did she know where to find you?" Simon completes her sentence for her. "She didn't. I found you." He produces a small flip-open wallet and holds it in front of Nadine's face. "DC Simon Waterhouse, Culver Valley Police."

Nadine laughs. "A detective? From the back of beyond, but still—why am I getting a visit from a detective? Whatever she's told you—"

"She hasn't been able to tell me anything because you haven't told her anything, but that's going to change. Today. Now. No more dropping hints and running away. The three of us are going to have a proper conversation. Can we come in?'

"No! You can piss off, is what you can do."

Simon grabs my left hand and pulls me forward. "Look—see this ring? It's an engagement ring. Looks pricey, doesn't it? Biggest diamond I've ever seen on a real person's finger." I wonder how many fake people's fingers he's seen. I wonder if I'll be wondering about fakeness for the rest of my life: fake fingers, fake fish allergies . . .

"I'm guessing you can work out what it means. Tom Rigbey asked Chloe to marry him last night and she said yes."

Nadine is staring at my ring as if it's a crushed cockroach.

Simon says, "Chloe didn't listen to your warning, evidently. If you want her to, you're going to need to tell her more. If you don't, I will."

Scorn contorts Nadine's face. "How can you tell her what you don't know?"

"I know enough. Speros, Jackson and Decker . . . and you're going to fill in the rest. Let us in."

What? Speros, Jackson, Decker? The names mean nothing to me. Nadine, who suddenly looks frightened, understands. I don't.

She opens the door wider and steps back so that her back is flat against the wall. Simon, still holding my arm, pulls me into the house.

There are no pleasantries, no offers of cups of tea or glasses of water. In silence, we proceed up the stairs to the first floor lounge. It's tidy, with beige walls, a wooden floor and white furniture—furry white poufs in front of the chairs instead of footstools. The fireplace is the smallest I've ever seen, and looks wrong. This is a modern room with a balcony overlooking the garden. It doesn't need and shouldn't have a fireplace.

There's a glass coffee table between Nadine's chair and where Simon and I are sitting. On it are some magazines and two bottles of nail varnish: one dark green and one silver. There are three framed prints on the walls, matching ones: cats with triangular, glittery faces. I've seen these pictures before on cards in shops. Maybe not these exact ones but the same kind.

"Go on," Simon says to Nadine. "Time to give Chloe the explanation she deserves. Tell her—tell us both—your story. The truth. Leave nothing out."

"It's difficult for me to talk about," she says.

"Yeah, I bet it is." Simon sounds unsympathetic. "Why don't you start with Speros? That was the first one, wasn't it? Then Jackson and Decker next. Then CamEgo. Where next, Nadine?"

Silence.

Questions are stampeding in my head, but I mustn't say anything. Simon is the questioner. He's made that very clear. I am the listener, passive and compliant, about to be rewarded with the truth. *Keep your mouth shut, Chloe.*

"Funny how you were so eloquent and articulate when you warned Chloe to stay away from Tom," says Simon. "You didn't tell her much, but what you said was powerful. Memorable. Yet now you can't seem to say anything at all. Why is that?"

"Someone please tell me what going on, before I go crazy," I blurt out. "What's Speros? Who are Jackson and Decker? Are those other companies Tom worked for? Did they get rid of him?"

Simon turns to face me. "Why do you ask that? Is it because I told you Tom had been fired?"

"Yes. And now you're mentioning company-sounding names I've never heard of."

"You're wrong, Chloe. You're too suggestible. If you think back over what I said at the market stall, you'll realize I never said that Tom had been fired from anywhere. He hasn't. He's never been anything but an exemplary employee."

"What? But you said—"

"I asked you if he'd said anything to you about being fired. I asked if he'd mentioned the circumstances in which he left either Sagentia or Intel."

"Yes, and you said Lorna's question was the right one, when she asked if he'd been sacked."

"It was the right one. I wanted to get you all thinking along those lines: people being fired."

"You also said sociopaths tend not to be able to hold down jobs for very long, and have to fake references to get new jobs."

"Yeah, I did. But I never said any of that applied to Tom Rigbey, did I?"

"I don't remember. I don't memorize every word you utter, I'm sorry."

"Take it from me," says Simon. "I didn't. Because Tom Rigbey has never been forcibly ejected from any company he's worked for. Tom Rigbey is not a sociopath. Yes, sociopaths often get fired. Who do you know that's been fired recently, Chloe? Anyone spring to mind?"

What could he mean?

Only one thing.

Having stopped for a second, the world starts to turn again, in a different direction.

"You," I breathe, staring at Nadine.

"At last." Simon sounds relieved. "Chloe Daniels, meet Nadine Caspian the sociopath."

Chapter 16

"I'm not any label that applies to a group of people," says Nadine. If she's shocked or hurt to be described as a sociopath, she doesn't show it. "I'm me—an individual."

"One who's been fired three times now," says Simon. "And for the same thing in all three cases. It's an unusual form of transgression, I'll grant you that. As you say: individual. At Speros Engineering, you picked on one Martin Kennett—like Tom Rigbey, Kennett was a man way above you in the office hierarchy. You were friendly and helpful to him to his face, but every so often you'd take someone aside—someone you thought might be about to get close to him, someone who seemed to think well of him—and you'd warn them about him. 'Keep away from Martin Kennett—he's bad news, seriously bad.' You probably put it more poetically, I'd imagine, since you described Tom Rigbey as a plague. You don't want to deny any of this?"

"No." Nadine smiles. "I warned people about Martin, yes. I think it's important to warn people, even if it's not what they want to hear. It's for their own good."

"You were fired from Speros because, although your hints gained some traction initially and some people did keep their distance from Kennett, you shared your poisonous warnings with one person too many. Eventually, someone with more-than-average confidence in their own opinion refused to be swayed, and instead thought, 'Hang on a minute. There's no way Martin Kennett's evil or dangerous, and no one should be trying to blacken another person's name at work without hard facts to back up her story.' I don't know who that person was, Nadine. The bloke I spoke to at Speros wouldn't tell me her name. Maybe you know it? Anyway, whatever her name was, she went to her boss and made a fuss. Martin Kennett versus Nadine Caspian became official and guess what? You had nothing to back up your claims and hints, did you? You were revealed for what you were. Are, I should say: a spiteful troublemaker who picks on innocent people at random, then warns others about them. That's *all* you do—but it's enough."

"Don't you think it's important to warn people against danger?" Nadine asks Simon, as if she's heard none of what he's been saying. "As a policeman, I'm sure you issue warnings all the time. Warnings are good for society, and for individuals."

"It's a clever tactic, if you want to destroy other people and their relationships," Simon goes on as if she hasn't spoken.

I've never heard a conversation like this before. For me to join in in any way feels impossible. Both Simon and Nadine seem to be trapped in their own private worlds, speaking but not hearing. Set apart, in two sealed bubbles, miles apart. I'm frozen, trying to listen hard and remember every word.

"Jackson and Decker, exactly the same story," says Simon. "This time it was the MD you selected as your victim, Iain Jackson. You took people into corners and advised them not to trust him, even with the smallest thing. You said it in a way that implied a detailed backstory, untold suffering . . . and it was bullshit. Lies. All made up. Iain Jackson might have done terrible things to people—anything's possible—but if he had, you knew nothing about them. You had no reason to think he was any more dangerous than anyone else at Jackson and Decker. As with Speros, you weren't quite subtle or selective enough. You told one person, eventually, who wasn't content to avoid Jackson from that moment on purely on your say-so. He made an issue of it, demanded proof, and you had none. He started to suspect you were the person everyone needed to be warned about. A short while later, you got fired for the second time. Then history repeated itself at CamEgo—your third sacking in four years."

Simon turns to me. "Chloe, when you heard Nadine had lost her job, you feared Tom had made it happen because you'd told him enough to make him fear she was onto him. Not true. There was nothing to be onto. Nadine was on her way to getting the boot anyway. Several people at CamEgo were wise to her antics, but it was the conversation you had with her on the stairs that speeded up the process."

"On . . . on the stairs?" I hear myself say. I didn't mention that to Simon—where we were when she said those horrible things. Someone else must have told him. He's clearly been thorough in his research.

"That's right. You were overheard, Nadine. On the other side of a thin wall was another flight of stairs leading up to the next floor. Someone coming down those stairs, another CamEgo employee, heard every slanderous word you said. He heard you describe Tom Rigbey as a plague in human form and, knowing this was as far from the truth as it's possible to be, he went to his line manager. Coincidentally, that person had been told only the day before about your campaign to badmouth Tom."

Nadine has started to look impatient. "I've done nothing worse than advise people to be careful, DC . . . I can't remember your surname."

"Waterhouse. Is that your best defense?"

"It's short and to the point."

"Yes, in keeping with your overall strategy," Simon agrees. "Say as little as possible. You don't need to kill, bomb, mutilate to have an effect. That would be too easy. Any fool armed with a weapon can wreak havoc—where's the challenge there? You do nothing but warn. If lives are destroyed as a result, it's so much more satisfying for you, because you've barely put yourself out at all. What's strange is that you can't see it's *your* life you're trashing. How many more times are you prepared to be fired? Why don't you just stop?"

Nadine leans forward and taps the glass coffee table with her fingernail. "Cite me one thing I've said that's factually untrue. All I did was express my own personal opinion to Chloe. I'm entitled to my opinion."

"It's not your true opinion," says Simon. "I think you go out of your way to pick blameless, good, decent people. That makes it more fun, does it? Luckily for the world, and unluckily for you, there are plenty of people who hear warnings like the kind you dish out and don't just think, 'No smoke without fire' and ostracize whoever you suggest. Luckily, Chloe chose to ignore you, and is now engaged to Tom Rigbey. She could see he was a decent guy, even if she couldn't immediately see what a toxic person you are."

"Toxic?" Nadine laughs. "Toxic because I warned her, as a friend would? Isn't that what we do when we care deeply about someone? Spot the dangers that might lie in store for them and warn them to take a different path? Warn them until they don't trust their own judgment anymore, and will take our word for anything? I'm sure you've done it, DC Simon—oh, yes, you have! You're doing it now: warning Chloe not to trust me. How's that any different to what I said to Chloe about Tom? You can't possibly know what kind of satisfying, meaningful friendship Chloe and I might have had if your 'toxic' slurs hadn't got in the way. Isn't that right, Chloe? Is there any point in my warning you now—don't trust DC Simon? No?"

Simon blinks at her a few times. Then he says, "It happened to you, didn't it? That's what's behind this. You were warned away from somebody. At work? In your love life? You listened, you heeded the warning, and you came to regret it bitterly. The person who gave you the advice might have done so because they cared—maybe too much—but they were wrong. You suffered as a result. You lost something."

Nadine's mouth flattens into a line. Is she even listening? She mutters, "Of course, you could argue that anyone who heeds a warning from a stranger deserves everything they get. If your theory about me is right—I'm not saying it is, but if it *were*—well, I'd be living proof of an important principle: trust your own judgment when it comes to those you care about. Don't trust strangers pushing slander. If your theory were true, DC Simon, which it isn't . . . then I set Chloe a test. And she passed."

"But you failed when it happened to you," Simon says. "You didn't trust your own judgment. And you've never forgiven yourself. Never got over it."

"Interesting story." Nadine looks away, toward the door to the balcony. "Also interesting that you feel free to make up stories about me while condemning me for doing the same thing—allegedly."

I clear my throat. "Nadine, if Simon's got you all wrong, tell me what it is about Tom that makes you think he's a plague and not to be trusted. It's your opinion—fine—but what are you basing it on?" I want something conclusive from her. Did she set me a test, which I passed, or offer me a chance to protect myself that I blindly ignored? What is her genuine opinion of Tom?

Why do you care? You trust Simon Waterhouse, don't you?

"I was just trying to warn you, Chloe," she snaps. "For your own sake. I wish I hadn't bothered."

The aggression in her voice throws me. She kept her tone civil, if chilly, for her dialogue with Simon, so why is she lashing out at me?

Because, if Simon's right, she can't forgive you—for being in the situation she was once in and choosing differently. She lost something. She suffered. You're engaged to Tom Rigbey, on your way to happy ever after. She sees you as her counterpart—in love, adoring, impressed by a brilliant man—and can't forgive you for being wiser than she was. Easier for her to forgive Simon, who has accused and exposed her.

"But why did you feel the need to warn me?" I persist. For some reason, in spite of everything, I want to give her one last chance. I don't want to condemn anybody on weak evidence. Not Tom, certainly, but no one else either.

"How can I talk to you now, Chloe?" Nadine demands, as if I've let her down. "How? You're engaged to him? You've made it very clear whose side you're on. Anything I said now would fall on deaf ears."

Simon stands up. "Let's go, Chloe. She won't tell you anything because there's nothing to tell."

"Chloe's not so sure about that, DC Simon. Are you, Chloe?"

"Yes," I say. "Yes, I am. Get some help. I'm sorry if you've had a bad experience, but it's not my fault, or Tom's. Stop trying to ruin other people's happiness."

"That's right," says Nadine bitterly as Simon and I turn to leave. "You tell yourself *I'm* the one doing that. You believe exactly what suits you, like everyone else does."

Chapter 17

"WHERE DO YOU want me to drop you?" Simon asks. We're in his car, driving away from St. Matthew's Gardens. *Thank God.*

"I don't," I say. "Just . . . drive around for a bit. I'm not ready to . . . I mean, I need to ask you some questions."

"Ask away," he says wearily. I ignore the tone and choose to notice only that I've been given official permission.

"You honestly believe Nadine Caspian is . . . what? A serial warner? That's it, all she does? She warns people about other people? Is that a thing? Have you ever known anyone else do that?"

Simon sighs. "No. It's a new one for me. But I've known lots of dysfunctional people who have taken something that wasn't a thing and never should have become one, and turned it into their own personal form of inflicting harm."

"All those questions you asked me about Tom—had he told me he'd been fired . . ."

"I wanted you to focus on what you knew for sure. You had no reason to think Tom had been fired. You knew that Nadine had—that other receptionist told you. I was hoping you'd figure out that, in the absence of any other certainties, that fact alone ought to make you more suspicious of Nadine than of Tom."

"And . . . when you said it was good that I'd had dinner with Tom and accepted his marriage proposal . . . when you told me to reply to his text as if nothing at all was wrong . . ."

"Yeah. I didn't want Tom to get wind of your suspicions—planted in your head by Nadine. Most people don't take kindly to be suspected of every heinous sin under the sun when they've never harmed anyone. I didn't want you to start acting cold and withdrawn and aloof with Tom in case it ruined a promising new relationship."

"I wish you'd told me as soon as you knew," I say, as we drive past the Vue cinema on East Road. "Why didn't you?"

"Once I knew the truth, I knew I needed to tell you, and I wanted to say it in front of Nadine, see how she'd react. Why would I go through the same spiel twice?"

"For the sake of my peace of mind," I say pointedly.

"I suppose," he concedes. I wait for an apology, but none arrives. I wonder if anyone has ever warned anyone to have nothing to do with DC Simon Waterhouse.

"Nadine's right about one thing," he says. "It's something people often do when they care about others, or imagine they do. They warn them. Maybe they shouldn't."

"Maybe not. Unless an enormous boulder is about to land on someone's head."

"You can't tell people how they ought to feel about other people," says Simon. "It doesn't work. Have you and Lorna been best friends for a long time?"

The mention of Lorna's name surprises me. For once, she wasn't in my thoughts at all.

"Yes. It feels like forever. Why?"

"No reason." Simon smiles. "Don't worry, I'm not going to warn you about her." He gives me an impenetrable look, then shakes his head.

"Because you don't think she's bad for me, or because Nadine Caspian's put you off warning anyone about anything ever?" I ask.

"I like your suspicious mind," he says. "I warn you: carry on like that and you might end up working for the police. She asked me to drop you off at her house—after our visit to Nadine."

"Who did? Lorna?"

He nods.

"No. Drop me off at my . . ." I change my mind mid-sentence. "Actually, can you drop me off at CamEgo? I want to see Tom, as soon as possible."

"No problem."

As I climb out of the car, my phone buzzes twice in my pocket. A text. I wait until I've waved Simon off, then pull out my phone, praying it's from Tom.

It is. Four words – "A mouthful of fish! T xx"—attached to a photo so unflattering that I'm amazed he dared send it. His mouth is wide open and there's half of what looks like a tuna sandwich stuffed inside it, hanging out because it won't all fit in.

It's not the salmon fillet from earlier, but I suppose tuna will suffice as evidence. Eating fish did happen and here's the picture to prove it: a gross one that would put many women off, perhaps, but not me.

I love Tom Rigbey, and I'm going to marry him. He could push a charity worker under a bus tomorrow, or have the flag of some unpronounceable country ruled by a dictator tattooed on his face and I would still love him every bit as much as I do now.

Did you love *THE WARNING*?

Sophie Hannah is back this summer with another dose of thrilling domestic suspense, full of psychological intrigue and surprise twists.

Turn the page for a sneak peek at

WOMAN WITH A SECRET

On sale August 4, 2015
From William Morrow

MEN SEEKING WOMEN

IntimateLinks > uk > all personals
Reply: 22547652@indiv.intimatelinksUK.org
Posted: 2013-07-04, 16:17PM GMT
Looking for a Woman with a Secret

LOCATION: WHEREVER YOU ARE

Hello, females!

Are you looking on here because you're hoping to find something that stands out from all the dull one-line I-want-a-blow-job-in-my-hotel-room-type adverts? Well, look no further. I'm different and this is different.

I'm not seeking casual sex or a long-term relationship. I've had plenty of the first in my time, and I've got one of the second that I'm happy with. Actually, I'm not looking for anything sexual or romantic. So what am I doing on Intimate Links? Well, as I'm sure you're aware if you're clever (and I suspect that the woman I am looking for is very bright), there are different kinds of intimacy. There's taking off your clothes and getting dirty with an illicit stranger, there's deep and meaningful love-making with a soulmate . . . and then there's the sort of intimacy that involves two people sharing nothing more than a secret. An important secret that matters to both of them.

Perhaps these two people have never met, or perhaps they know each other but not very well. Either way, they can only establish a bond of common knowledge once the one who has the information has given it to the one who needs it. Think of the rush of relief you'd experience if you shared your burden, after the agony of prolonged silence with the secret eating away at you . . . If you're the person I'm looking for, you'll be desperate to confide in someone.

That's where I come in. I'm your confidant, ready and eager to listen. Are you the keeper of the secret I'm waiting to be told?

Let's find out by asking a question that only the person I'm looking for would be able to answer. It will make no sense to anyone else. You'll have to bear with me. Before I get to the question part, I'll need to lay out the scenario.

Picture a room in a large Victorian house: a spacious, high-ceilinged first-floor bedroom that's used as a study. There are overstuffed built-in bookshelves in this room, a pale blue and brown jukebox with curved edges that has a vintage look about it and is much more beautiful than the kind you sometimes see in pubs, an armchair, a filing cabinet, a long desk with square wooden legs and a green glass top that has a laptop computer at its centre. The computer is neither open nor closed. Its lid is at a forty-five-degree angle, as if someone has tried half-heartedly to push it shut but it hasn't gone all the way. The laptop is surrounded on all sides by cheap-looking biros, empty and half-empty coffee mugs, and scattered papers: handwritten notes, ideas jotted down.

Pushed back from the desk is a standard black office-style swivel chair, and lolling in the chair, his head leaning to the left, is a dead man. While alive, he was well known and—though this might well have nothing to do with anything—strikingly attractive in a stubbly, cowboy-without-a-hat kind of way. If I were to include his name in this account, I think most people would have heard of him. Some of you might shudder and say, 'Oh, not that vile bigot!' or, more light-heartedly, 'Not that ridiculous attention-seeker!' Others would think, 'Oh, I love him – he says all the things I'm too scared to say.' Our dead body is (was) somebody who inspired strong feelings, you see. So strong that he got himself murdered.

How was he killed? Well, this is the interesting part. The murder process comprised several stages. First, he was immobilised. His arms were pulled behind the back of his chair and taped together at the wrists. The same was done to his ankles, which were taped together round the pole of the chair's base, beneath the seat. Then his murderer stood behind him and brought a heavy object down on his head, rendering him unconscious. The police found this object on the floor beside the dead man's desk: it was a metal kitchen-knife sharpener. It didn't kill our well-known man (the pathologist told the police after examining the body), though it would have made an excellent murder-by-bludgeoning weapon, being more than heavy enough to do the job. However, it seems that although the killer was happy to use the knife sharpener to knock his victim out, he did not wish to use it to murder him.

There was a knife in the room too, but it had not been used to stab the dead man. Instead, it was stuck to his face with parcel tape. Specifically, it was stuck to his closed mouth, completely covering it. The tape—of which there was plenty—also completely covered the lower part of the murder victim's face, including his nose, causing him to suffocate to death. The knife's blade, flat against the dead man's mouth, was sharp. Forensics found evidence that it had been sharpened in the room, and detectives suspect that this happened after the victim was bound to the chair and unconscious.

Above the fireplace, on the wall between two bookshelf-filled alcoves, someone had written in big red capital letters, 'HE IS NO LESS DEAD.' I imagine that the first police to arrive at the scene took one look at that and leaped to a mistaken conclusion: that the red words had been written in the victim's blood. Then, seconds later, they might have noticed a tin of paint and a red-tipped brush on the floor and made a more informed guess that turned out to be correct: the words on the wall were written in paint. Dulux's Ruby Fountain 2, for anyone who is interested in the details and doesn't already know them.

Detectives examined the dead man's laptop, I assume. They would have found this surprisingly easy because the killer had red-painted, 'Riddy111111,' on a blank sheet of white A4 paper that was lying on the desk. This was the well-known man's password and would have led police straight to his hushmail inbox. There they'd have found a new, unopened message from a correspondent by the name of No Less Dead, with an email address to match. There were no words in the message, only a photograph of someone standing in the room beside the unconscious, not-yet-deceased victim, wearing what looked like a protective suit from a Hollywood film about biological outbreaks—the sort that covers the head and body of the person wearing it. The killer's eyes would presumably have been visible if he or she hadn't taken care to turn away from the camera; as it was, the picture showed a completely unidentifiable person with one outstretched arm (for the taking of the photo), holding aloft a knife in his or her other hand, above the unconscious man's chest, in a way designed to suggest that a stabbing was imminent. The knife in the photograph was the same one (or identical to the one) that ended up taped to the murder victim's face, suffocating him rather than spilling his blood.

And now the question is coming up, so pay attention, ladies! (Actually, it's questions, plural.)

The murderer planned the crime in advance. It was about as premeditated as a killing can be. It involved bringing to the crime scene a knife, a knife sharpener, parcel tape, red paint, a paintbrush and a bio-hazard suit. The killer obviously knew the deceased's computer password. How? There was no evidence of a break-in. Did her victim let her in? (I'm saying 'her' because that's my hunch: that it was a woman. Maybe it was you?) Did the well-known man say to her, 'Go on, then: bind me to my chair, knock me out and kill me'? That seems unlikely. Maybe the killer pretended it was some sort of erotic game, or maybe I'm only speculating along these lines because Intimate Links is the perfect place to do so – the online home of sexual game-players of all kinds.

The most puzzling question is this: why arrive at the victim's house with a knife and a knife sharpener when you have no intention of stabbing him? Why sharpen that knife at the crime scene if all you're going to do is tape it, flat, against his face? For that purpose, the knife would work just as effectively if its blade were blunt.

Or, looking at it another way . . . if you've got a newly sharpened knife, and you've covered your clothing to protect it from blood splashes, and if, coincidentally, you also want to write a strange message in big red letters on the wall, why not stab the guy and use his blood to write with? Because you particularly want to suffocate him? Then why not do it more straightforwardly, with, say, a plastic bag over his head, taped round his neck to make it airtight? Why use a knife at all?

For some reason, you wanted to kill this man with a sharp knife, but you didn't want to stab him. Why not? And the photograph you emailed—what's that about? What are you trying to communicate? Is it 'Look, I could so easily have stabbed him, but I didn't'?

I realise I've slipped into using 'you' when I talk about the murderer, rather than 'she', or 'he or she'. I'm sorry. I'm not accusing you of killing anybody. Maybe you're not the murderer of the well-known man. You might be someone who wishes he were still alive, someone who loves him, or once did—a lover, a close friend. I'm really not sure. All I know is that you're reading this and you know the answers to the questions I'm asking. You desperately want to tell someone what you know.

I'm the person to trust with the information. I've taken a huge risk in sharing so many secrets, in the hope of eliciting a reply from you. So, please, contact me. I'm waiting, and I promise I won't judge you. Whatever you've done, you had your reasons. I am ready to listen and understand.

Looking forward to hearing from you soon.

C (for Confidant) x

• Location: Wherever You Are
• It's NOT OK to contact this poster with services or other commercial interests
Posted: 2013-07-04, 16:17PM GMT

Chapter 1

IT CAN'T BE him. All policemen wear high-visibility jackets these days. Lots must have sand-colored hair that's a little bit wavy. In a minute he'll turn round and I'll see his face and laugh at myself for panicking.

Don't turn around, unless you're someone else. Be someone else. Please.

I sit perfectly still, try not to notice the far-reaching reverberations of every heartbeat. There is too much distance trapped in me. Miles. I can't reach myself. A weird illusion grips me: that I am my heart and my car is my chest, and I'm shaking inside it.

Seconds must be passing. Not quickly enough. Time is stuck. I stare at the clock on my dashboard and wait for the minute to change. At last, 10:52 becomes 10:53 and I'm relieved, as if it could have gone either way.

Crazy.

He's still standing with his back to me. So many details are the same: his hair, his height, his build, the yellow jacket with "POLICE" printed on it . . .

If it's him, that means I must be doing something wrong, and I'm not. I'm definitely not. There's no reason for him to reappear in my life; it wouldn't be fair, when I'm trying so hard. Out of everyone sitting in their cars in this line of traffic, I must be among the most blameless, if I'm being judged on today's behavior alone: a mother driving to school to deliver her son's forgotten gym bag. I could have said, "Oh well, he'll just have to miss games, or wear his school uniform," but I didn't. I knew Ethan would hate those two options equally, so I canceled my hair appointment and set off back to school, less than an hour after I'd gotten home from dropping the children off there. Willingly, because I care about my son's happiness.

Which means this has to be a different policeman up ahead. It can't be him. It was my guilt that drew him to me last time. Today, I'm innocent. I've been innocent for more than three weeks.

Drew him to you?

All right, I'm guilty of superstitious idiocy, but nothing else. If it's him, he's here on Elmhirst Road by chance—pure coincidence, just as it was last time we met. He's a police officer who works in Spilling; Elmhirst Road is in Spilling: his presence here, for reasons that have nothing to do with me, is entirely plausible.

Rationally, the argument stands up, but I'm not convinced.

Because you're a superstitious fool.

If it's him, that means I'm still guilty, deep down. If he sees me . . .

I can't let that happen. His eyes on me, even for a second, would act as a magnet, dragging the badness inside me up to the surface of my skin, making it spill out into the open; it would propel me back to where I was when he first found me: the land of the endangered.

I don't deserve that. I have been good for three weeks and four days. Even in the privacy of my mind, where any transgressions would be unprovable, I haven't slipped up. Once or twice my thoughts have almost broken free of my control, but I've been disciplined about slamming down the barriers.

Turn around, quick, before he does.

Can I risk it?

A minute ago, there were at least fifteen cars between mine and where he's standing on the pavement, a few hundred meters ahead. There are still about ten, at a rough guess. If one of the drivers in front of me would do a U-turn and go back the way they came, I'd do the same, but he's more likely to notice me if I'm the first to do it. He might recognize my car, remember the make and model—maybe even the license plate. Not that he's turned around yet, but he could be about to. Any second now . . .

He'd wonder why I was doubling back on myself. The traffic isn't at a standstill. True, we're crawling along, but it's unlikely to take me more than ten minutes to get past whatever's causing the delay. All I can see from my car is a female police officer in the road, standing up straight, then bobbing down out of sight; standing up again, bobbing down again. I think she must be saying something to the driver of each car that passes. There's another male officer too, on the pavement, talking to . . .

Not him. Talking to a man who, please God, isn't him.

Inhale. Long and deep.

I can't do it. The presence of the right words in my mind is not enough to drive away the panic, not when I'm breathing jagged and fast like this.

I wish I could work out what's going on up there. It's probably something dull and bureaucratic. Once before, I was stopped by fluorescent-jacketed police—three of them, like today—who were holding up traffic on the Rawndesley Road as part of a survey about driver behavior. I've forgotten what questions they asked me. They were boring, and felt pointless at the time. I remember thinking, My answers will be of no benefit to anyone, and answering politely anyway.

The car in front of mine moves forward at the exact same moment that the policeman with his back to me turns his head. I see him in profile, only for a second, but it's enough. I make a choking noise that no one hears but me. I'm embarrassed anyway.

It's him.

No choice, then. Driving past him is unthinkable—no way of avoiding being seen by him if his colleague stops my car to speak to me—so I'll have to turn around. I edge forward and swerve to the right, waiting for a gap in the oncoming traffic on the other side of the road so that I can escape.

Please. I'll feel OK as soon as I'm traveling away from him and not towards him.

I edge out farther. Too far, over the white line, where there's no room for me. A blue Toyota beeps its horn as it flies past, the driver's open mouth an angry blur. The noise is long and drawn out: the sound of a long grudge, not a fleeting annoyance, though I'm not sure if I'm still hearing its echo or only remembering it. Shock drums a rhythmic beat through my body, rising up from my chest into my throat and neck, pulsing down to my stomach. It pounds in my ears, in the skin of my face; I can even feel it in my hair.

There's no way a noise like that car horn isn't going to make a policeman—any policeman—turn around and see what's going on.

It's OK. It's fine. Nothing to worry about. How likely is it that he'd remember my car registration? He'll see a silver Audi and think nothing of it. He must see them all the time.

I keep my head facing away from him, my eyes fixed on the other side of the road, willing a gap to appear. One second, two seconds, three . . .

Don't look. He'll be looking by now. No eye contact, that's what matters. As long as you don't see him seeing you . . .

At last, there's space for me to move out. I spin the car around and drive back along Elmhirst Road towards Spilling town center, seeing all the same things that I saw a few minutes ago, except in reverse order: the garden center, the Arts Barn, the house with the mint-green camper van parked outside it that looks like a Smeg fridge turned on its side, with wheels attached. These familiar objects and buildings seemed ordinary and unthreatening when I drove past them a few minutes ago. Now there's something unreal about them. They look staged. Complicit, as if they're playing a sinister game with me, one they know I'll lose.

Feeling hot and dizzy, I turn left into the library parking lot and take the first space I see: what Adam and I have always called "a golfer's space" because the symbol painted in white on the concrete looks more like a set of golf clubs than the stroller it's supposed to be.

I open the car door with numb fingers that feel as if they're only partly attached to my body and find myself gasping for air. I'm burning hot, dripping with sweat, and it has nothing to do with the weather.

Why do I still feel like this? I should have been able to leave the panic behind, on Elmhirst Road. With him.

Get a grip. Nothing bad has actually happened. Nothing at all has happened.

"You're not parking there, are you? I hope you're going to move."

I look up. A young woman with auburn hair and the shortest bangs I've ever seen is staring at me. I assume the question came from her, since there's no one else around. Explaining my situation to her is more than I can manage at the moment. I can form the words in my mind, but not in my mouth. *I'm not exactly parking. I just need to sit here for a while, until I'm safe to drive again. Then I'll go.*

I'm so caught up in the traumatic nothing that happened to me on Elmhirst Road that I only realize she's still there when she says, "That space is for mums and babies. You've not got a baby with you. Park somewhere else!"

"Sorry. I . . . I will. I'll move in a minute. Thanks."

I smile at her, grateful for the distraction, for a reminder that this is my world and I'm still in it: the world of real, niggly problems that have to be dealt with in the present.

"What's wrong with right now?" she says.

"I just . . . I'm not feeling . . ."

"You're in a space for mothers with babies! Are you too stupid to read signs?" Her aggression is excessive—mysteriously so. "Move! There's at least fifty other free spaces."

"And at least twenty-five of those are mother-and-child spaces," I say, looking at all the straight yellow lines on the concrete running parallel to my car, with nothing between them. "I'm not going to deprive anyone of a space if I sit here for another three minutes. I'm sorry, but I'm not feeling great."

"You don't know who's going to turn up in a minute," says my persecutor. "The spaces might all fill up." She pushes at her toothbrush-bristle bangs with her fingers. She seems to want to flick them to one side and hasn't worked out that they're too short to go anywhere; all they can do is lie flat on her head.

"Do you work at the library?" I ask her. I've never seen a Spilling librarian wearing stiletto-heeled crocodile-skin ankle boots before, but I suppose it's possible.

"No, but I'll go and get someone who does if you don't move."

What is she, then? A recreational protester whose chosen cause is the safeguarding of mother-and-child parking spaces for those who deserve them? She has no children with her, or any books, or a bag big enough to contain books. What's she doing here in the library parking lot?

Get the bitch, says the voice in my head that I mustn't listen to. *Bring her down.*

"Two questions for you," I say coolly. "Who the hell do you think you are, and who the hell are you?"

"It doesn't matter! What matters is, you're in the wrong space!"

"Read the sign," I tell her. To save her the trouble of turning around, I read it aloud to her, "'These spaces are reserved for people with children.' That includes me. I have two children. I can show you photos. Or my C-section scar, if you'd prefer?"

"It *means* for people who've got children with them *in the car,* as you well know! Shall I go and get the library manager?"

"Fine by me." I'm starting to feel better, thanks to this woman. I'm enjoying myself. "She can tell us what she thinks the sign means, and I'll tell her what it says, and explain the difference. 'People with children' means 'parents.' Those with offspring, progeny, descendants: the non-childless. There's nothing in the wording of that sign that specifies where the children need to be, geographically, at this precise moment. If it said, 'This space is reserved for people who have their kids with them *right here and now in this library parking lot,'* I could see a justification for moving. Since it doesn't . . ." I shrug.

"Right," Short Bangs snaps at me. "You wait there!"

"What, in the parking space you're so keen for me to vacate?" I call after her as she stomps toward the library. "You want me to stay in it now?"

She makes an obscene finger gesture over her shoulder.

I'd like to wait and argue with the librarian—all the librarians, if possible—but the return of my normal everyday self has brought with it the memory of why I left the house: to deliver Ethan's sports bag to school. I should get on with it; I know he'll worry until he has it in his hands.

Reluctantly, I slam my car door shut, pull out of the library parking lot and head for the Silsford Road. I can get to the school via Upper Heckencott, I think. It's a ridiculously long-winded way of getting there, involving skinny, winding lanes that you have to reverse back along for about a mile if you meet a car coming in the opposite direction, but you generally don't. And it's the only route I can think of that doesn't involve driving down Elmhirst Road.

I check my watch: 11:10 A.M. I pull my phone out of my bag, ring school, ask them to tell Ethan not to worry and that I'm on my way. All of this I do while driving, knowing I shouldn't, hoping I'll get away with it. I wonder if it's possible, simultaneously, to be a good mother and a bad person: someone who enjoys picking fights with strangers in parking lots, who lies, who gets into trouble with the police and nearly ruins her life and the life of her family, who thinks, Fuck you, every time anyone points out what the rules are and that she's breaking them.

I blow a long sigh out of the open window, as if I'm blowing out smoke. Ethan deserves a mother with no secrets, a mother who can drive to school without needing to hide from anyone. Instead, he has me. Soon he'll have his gym bag too.

It could be worse for him. I'm determined to make it better, to make myself better.

Three weeks and four days. A verbal scrap with a self-righteous idiot doesn't count as a lapse, I decide, at the same time as I tell myself that I mustn't let it happen again—that I must be more humble in future, even if provoked. Less combative, more . . . ordinary. Like the other school mums. Though less dull than them, I hope. Never the sort of person who would say, "A home isn't a home without a dog," or, "I don't know why I bother going to the gym—forty minutes on the treadmill and what do I do as soon as I get home? Raid the biscuit tin!"

As safe and honorable as those women, but more exciting. Is that possible?

I like to have it both ways; that's my whole problem, in a nutshell.

AS SOON AS I arrive at school, I am presented with an opportunity to put my new non-confrontational manner to the test. "We discourage parents from going into classrooms," a receptionist I've never seen before tells me, standing in front of me to block my way.

Since when? I've been into both Sophie's and Ethan's classrooms many times. No one's ever complained.

"It's emotionally disruptive for the children if a parent suddenly pops up during lesson time," she explains. "Some of them think, Oh look, Mum or Dad's here—they can take me home, and get very upset when Mum or Dad disappears again, leaving them behind."

"I promise you Ethan won't be upset." I smile hopefully at

her. "He'll just be pleased and relieved to have his gym bag." *And, obviously, since he wants it for games this afternoon, he won't, on having it handed to him, expect to leave school immediately and miss the PE lesson that he needs it for, you stupid cow.* "There's really no downside to letting me take it to him myself, honestly," I add in what I hope is a wholly positive tone of voice. "It'll save you a job too."

"Nicki!" a high-pitched female voice calls out, one that would be better suited to a cheerleader than a head teacher. *Correction: headmistress.*

I sag with relief, knowing that everything is about to be all right. Kate Zilber is here: five foot short, petite as a ten-year-old, the most indiscreet person in professional employment that I've ever met. Kate refuses to be referred to as "principal" or "head"; "headmistress" is her title, prominently engraved on the sign on her office door, and she insists that people use it. She once described herself to me as a megalomaniac; I soon discovered that she wasn't exaggerating.

"Is that Ethan's PE bag?" she says. "It's OK, Izzie, we can bend the rules on this occasion. Actually, I can bend them whenever it suits me, since I run the place—perk of the job. We don't want Nicki worrying about whether the bag was safely delivered, do we?"

Izzie shrugs ungraciously and returns to her desk.

Kate pulls me out of the office and into an empty corridor. Once we're alone, she says, "And the chances of it being safely delivered by Izzie are slim. She's a lobotomy on legs."

"Really?" I must stop questioning everything she says. I keep assuming she's joking, but she never is. I'm not used to people who work in elementary schools speaking their minds in the way Kate Zilber does. Still, Freeth Lane is well known to be the best independent school in the Culver Valley, and Kate's the person responsible for that. She could probably pelt the parents and governors with rotten eggs and get away with it.

"Quick pep talk for you." She gives me a stern look. "If you want to take Ethan his gym bag because you trust no one else to do the job properly, fine. But if there's an element of wanting to get a quick glimpse of him to reassure yourself that he's OK . . . not so fine."

"Why not?" I ask.

"If you indulge your own anxiety, you'll make Ethan's worse. He needs his gym bag; you've brought it in—problem solved." She squeezes my arm. "There's no need for you to see him, Nicki. You'll only read unhappiness into his expression, whether it's there or not, and work yourself up into a state. If he smiles at you, you'll worry he's putting on a brave face in front of his new friends. If he doesn't smile, you'll imagine he's in the grip of a powerful inner torment. Am I right?"

I sigh. "Probably."

"How about I take him his gym bag instead?" she suggests. "I'm the most reliable person on the planet. You know that, right? I'm even more efficient than you."

"All right." I smile and hand her the bag. For some reason, this tiny, shrewd, girly-voiced woman I barely know has a talent for very quickly making me feel ten times better. Every time she does, I can't help thinking of Melissa, who has the opposite effect and is my closest friend.

"Thank you." Kate turns to walk away, then turns back. "Ethan really will be fine, you know. He'll be as happy here as Sophie—you wait and see. Some children take longer than others to form emotional attachments and adapt to a new environment, that's all. The other kids are really rallying round, looking after him—this term even more than last. It's sweet. He's made so many new friends."

"Ethan's always been more sensitive than Sophie," I say. "He doesn't handle change well." *And his mother, knowing this, took him away from the school where he was happy. Two terms later, he still tells me at least once a week that he'll never love this school as much as his old one—that however many friends he makes, Oliver-who-he-left-behind-in-London will always be his true best friend, even if he never sees him again.*

"Nicki." Another stern look. "Ethan's fine. He occasionally gets anxious about things. Lots of kids do. It's really nothing serious. Your anxiety, on the other hand . . . You should take yourself to a head doctor, lady," she concludes affectionately.

"Kate, I—" I break off. What am I thinking? I can't tell her anything. I can't tell anyone, ever.

"What?"

"Nothing."

"Bugger 'nothing.' You can't start and not finish. Tell me or I'll expel your children."

"I've . . . been under a lot of pressure recently, that's all. I'm not normally so twitchy."

Kate raises a plucked eyebrow. "Don't fob me off, Nicki. That wasn't what you were going to say."

The urge to tell her—something, anything—is overwhelming.

"I lied to you."

"Ooh! This sounds promising." She moves closer, rubbing her hands together. No one else I know would react so enthusiastically to hearing they'd been deceived. *If only they would*. "Lied to me about what?"

"First time I came in to look round," I say, "you asked me why we wanted to leave London and move to Spilling."

"And you said what so many people who have moved from London say: better schools, bigger garden, cleaner air, perfect rural childhood, yada yada. Whenever parents tell me that, I think, Ha, just wait till your fourteen-year-old's roaming those big green fields you prize so highly, off his tits on illegal substances because there's no subway to take him anywhere worth going, and absolutely nothing to do in his local idyll."

I laugh. "Are you this frank with all the parents?"

Kate considers my question, then says, "I tone it down a bit for the squeamish ones. So, come on—the lie?"

"My real reason for moving here was entirely selfish, nothing to do with fresher air and bigger gardens. I wasn't thinking about my children, or my husband. Only myself."

"Well . . . good," says Kate.

"Good?"

"Absolutely. It's when we imagine we know how others feel and presume to know what's best for them that mistakes are made. Whereas no one knows our own needs better than us." She glances at her watch. "Looking after number one's not as daft a policy as it sounds: make the only person happy that you can, let everyone else do the same and take care of themselves. So why did you want to move to Spilling?"

I shake my head, look away. "It doesn't matter. It stopped being relevant shortly after we got here anyway. Sod's Law. I just wanted you to know: that's the reason I get anxious about Ethan."

"I get it," says Kate. "His suffering is your punishment. You don't believe you can avoid retribution for being as selfish as you've been, therefore Ethan must be suffering horribly?"

"Something like that," I mutter.

"I wouldn't think that way if I were you. Women need to be ruthlessly selfish. You know why? Because men are, and so are children. Both will turn you into their slave unless you give back as good as you get on the selfish front." I find myself looking at her left hand to see if she's wearing a wedding band; I've never noticed, and her name gives nothing away: she's Dr. Zilber, not Miss or Mrs.

She is wearing a wedding ring. A thin one—either white gold or platinum. The skin around it is pink, chapped and flaky, as if she's allergic to it.

"Listen, Nicki—much as I'd love to pry further into your secret reason for moving here, I'd better get on. There are people still on my staff who belong in the welfare line." She nods towards Izzie. "I can't rest until that's rectified. But first stop: Ethan's bag."

I thank her, and return to my car feeling more optimistic than I have for a while.

Maybe nothing all that terrible has happened to me. Maybe I'm not the guiltiest woman in the world. If I told

Kate, she might laugh and say, "God, what a story!" in an appreciative way. I'm so used to Melissa's harsh glare and pursed lips and, more recently, her refusal to listen, but she is only one person. *The wrong person to try and share a secret with, if the secret's anything more controversial than 'This is what I've bought so-and-so for their birthday—don't tell them.'*

The conclusion I've been strenuously trying to avoid reaching glows in neon in my brain: I need to give up on Melissa and find myself a new best friend. I can't get away from her—she's managed to tie us together forever, even if that wasn't her intention—but I can demote her in my mind to "acquaintance"; she'll never know I've done it, if I'm still friendly on the surface.

Is there a website, I wonder: newbestfriend.com? If there is, it's probably full of people trying to turn it non-platonic, looking for "fuck buddies" or "friends with benefits."

Kate Zilber wouldn't have let a run-in with a policeman stop her from doing what she wanted and needed to do. She wouldn't have been doing it in the first place unless she'd decided it was OK, and she wouldn't have been terrified and ashamed if caught. I doubt she'd have disappeared from Gavin's life with no word or explanation, as I did.

The fairest thing to do, for his sake and my family's— that's what I told myself.

Liar. Coward.

I owe him an explanation. For whatever reason, however stupid and crazy it was, he was significant to me for a while. He mattered. I think I mattered to him too.

I drive along the Silsford Road with the window open,

thinking about the possibility of contacting him now. Could I extend my definition of being good to include emailing him just once more, to tell him that my disappearance wasn't his fault, that he did nothing wrong?

No. It wouldn't be only once. He'd hook you again.

Cutting off from Gavin took all my willpower; I might not have the strength to do it a second time.

I decide to allow myself the luxury of not deciding immediately. I want to cling to the possibility—not of going back to how it was, but of one last communication, to end things in a proper way. I know better than anyone that sometimes a possibility is enough to keep a person going, even if it never becomes a reality.

Will Gavin still be checking, three weeks and four days after he last heard from me, or will he have given up by now? If it had been the other way around and he'd suddenly stopped emailing me, how soon would I have stopped looking to see if he'd written?

The phone's ringing as I pull up outside my house. I grab my bag, lock the car door and fumble with the front-door key, knowing the call will be about Ethan. Something's happened: he's sobbing, locked in a bathroom stall. Or there's a problem with his gym bag—something's missing. How sure am I that I put all the right things in?

Let him be OK and I swear I won't email Gavin, or even think about it any more.

I run into the living room and grab the phone, wondering why I persist in offering God these phony deals. If He exists, He must be reasonably intelligent—maybe not the academic four-A*s-at-A-level kind of clever, but powerfully intuitive, and with a deep understanding of people. He must have spotted the pattern by now: I never stick to my side of the bargains I make with Him. Time and time again, He goes easy on me and I think, Phew, and forget about what I promised I'd do in return, or invent a loophole to let myself off the hook.

I pick up the phone. "Hello?"

"Is that Mrs. Clements?"

"Yes, speaking."

"It's Izzie here, from Freeth Lane. We just met, when you came in before?"

"Is Ethan OK?" I resent the time it takes me to ask: endless stretched-out seconds of not knowing.

"Oh." Izzie sounds surprised. "I don't know."

"What do you mean, you don't know?" I snap.

"I assume he's all right. I haven't heard that he isn't."

"So you're not phoning about Ethan?"

"No."

I exhale slowly as I fall into a chair. "Right. So what can I do for you?"

"It's Sophie."

Sophie, who's never problematic in any way, who I don't need to worry about. I take her well-being for granted. I feel as if my heart has been lobbed at the wall of my gut, feel it sliding slowly downward, flattened by dread.

The children of guilty mothers, hostages to karma, always in imaginary peril that feels so real, so asked for . . .

"She's been sick," says Izzie. "She seems fine now, and she

says she wants to stay for the rest of the day, but it's policy to let parents know."

"I'm coming in now to see her," I say. "Tell her I'm on my way." I'm not taking the word of Lobotomy Izzie when it comes to the health of my daughter; I want to see for myself if Sophie's well enough to stay at school. Which means driving the round trip, yet again. And then again at the end of the day, either to pick up both children or, if I bring Sophie back with me early, to pick up Ethan. Fleetingly, I consider collecting them both now to save me having to drive back to school later for the fourth time in one day, but then I realize I can't make Ethan miss games, not after I've taken in his bag; he'll be looking forward to playing football or cricket or whatever it is, expecting the rest of his day to unfold predictably and without incident.

I decide that I'll be brave and try the Elmhirst Road route again. Getting to Sophie as quickly as possible matters more than my fear. If the sand-haired policeman is still there, I'll stay calm and pretend not to recognize him. Or maybe I'll wink at him. I can imagine Kate Zilber doing that. Winking isn't illegal. He wouldn't be able to warn me or threaten me. A wink proves nothing, and in any case, there has been nothing to prove since I turned good.

THE ROUTINE WHEN Sophie and Ethan get in from school at the end of the day is always the same. Panting and groaning, they shrug and wriggle their way out of their coats and shoes in the hall, as if divesting themselves of chains that have bound them for decades, before making a dash for the living room and slamming the door. They have an urgent appointment with the television that nothing would induce them to miss.

I am left to pick up the discards from the hall floor and throw them, in a big pile glued together by wet mud from the soles of football boots, into the coat cupboard; it's mess relocation rather than tidying up. Adam is patient and always waits until the cupboard's interior is indistinguishable from a compost heap before he complains. When he does, I either say, "I know. Sorry—I'll sort it out tomorrow," or I snap, "If you don't like it, do something about it," depending on my mood.

The CBBC channel starts to chatter mid-sentence. That's my cue to pour the juice and make the toast. Once they're on the kitchen table, I call out, "Snack's ready!"

"Bring it in here!" Sophie yells. She is more vocally militant than her brother, who is happy to be represented by her in all parent-child disputes.

"No!" I shout back.

"Yes! Remember, I was sick! I feel a bit weak!"

"You *were* sick—you're not now!" Nor was she when I arrived at school to check on her; she looked at me as if I were crazy, told me she had no intention of coming home with me and turned back to her friends. I left empty-handed, a person-with-children temporarily without her children, just as I was this morning in the library parking lot. It was only on my fourth and final trip to school that I came away with what I wanted: Sophie and Ethan in the back seat, and an overwhelming feeling of relief. I can't fully relax unless they're under the same roof as me; that's been true since we moved here from London.

Kate Zilber's right: I should probably get some therapy. I'm too anxious. Once, waiting to collect the children at the end of the day, I started to have palpitations because a man looked at me in a way that made me feel uncomfortable: a long-drawn-out superior smirk. He's one of the school's most pleased-with-himself Flash Dads. I often see him leaning against his expensive-looking blue BMW in the part of the playground where the showiest parents always wait. His hair is subtly streaked. It looks deliberate, which I know I shouldn't disapprove of, but I do. There are some things men just shouldn't do, and streaked hair is right up there alongside cosmetic pubic-hair removal. Though I've never seen his child or children, I enjoy imagining them as rebellious teenagers, covered with tattoos and piercings that spell out, "My dad's an utter cock."

"Please, Mum!" Sophie yells from the lounge.

I could refuse again, but what's the point? I'll give in eventually; I always do. I don't know why I bother going through the daily ritual of putting the plates and glasses down on the table in front of two chairs. I think it's because I like the idea of my children coming into the kitchen and chatting to me, so I create the conditions that will make it possible. Seeing the toast and juice neatly laid out on the table makes me feel like a proper mother.

We don't have many rules in our house. The few we do have—like no eating in the living room—are broken every day. Adam thinks it's stupid and inconsistent to ban things we disapprove of and then allow them to happen anyway. I'm torn. I admire people who don't allow themselves to be constrained by rules, and cheer inwardly every time my kids demonstrate that they have no intention of obeying me.

If I believed myself to be a fine, upstanding pillar of the community with a strong moral code, I might feel differently. Who am I to tell anyone how they ought to behave?

I take the toast and juice into the living room. Sophie tells me to "Shh" before I've said a word. Her eyes are glued to the television screen, as are Ethan's. I say, "Thank you, darling mother," loudly before leaving the room.

"Yeah, thanks, Mum," says Ethan. Three whole words. Amazing. He and Sophie tend to lose the ability to speak for about an hour and a half after they get home from school. They find their voices again at suppertime, after which we usually can't shut them up until bedtime.

Having delivered the snack, I pull the living room door closed behind me and hover in the hall, not sure what I'm going to do next. I have a strong suspicion, but that's not the same as being sure.

I should get to work in the kitchen. The dishwasher needs unloading and reloading before I can start cooking.

I shouldn't, definitely mustn't, email Gavin.

But you will. You're about to.

Breaking other people's rules might be commendably independent-minded, but breaking your own, which you made willingly, to protect yourself and your family? What kind of fool does that?

I want to continue to believe in the fantasy that I have a choice, but it doesn't feel true. The decision has been made, in the shadowy part of me that logic never reaches, where a force far greater than my willpower is in charge.

I look at my watch. Adam will be home in about half an hour. If I don't do it now, I won't have another chance until tomorrow.

Too long to wait.

As I run upstairs to our spare room, which houses the family computer, I wonder how I've managed to resist doing this for so long. Three weeks and four days. Until I saw that policeman again today, I was finding it easy to be good. The shock of my first meeting with him was all the motivation I needed. I don't understand why a second almost-encounter with him has driven me in the opposite direction.

You can still do the right thing. Sending one quick explanatory email for politeness's sake isn't the same as starting it up again.

It's what I should have done all along, instead of my cowardly vanishing act.

I close the spare-room door behind me, making sure I've shut it properly and not just pushed it to, and sit down at the desk. This will be the first time I've opened my secret Hushmail account since my first run-in with the policeman. I've been scared of discovering that Gavin's emailed me, scared I wouldn't have the strength to delete his message without reading it.

I type in my password, my heart beating like the wings of a trapped bird in my ears and throat, and prepare to confront my greatest fear: an empty inbox. What if he hasn't been in touch for the whole three weeks and four days that I haven't contacted him? That would mean that he was never as keen as I thought he was.

Good. It's good if he's not keen. It's good because we're over.

Though we never agreed on it in so many words, we operated a strict 'turns' system throughout our correspondence, both of us always waiting for a reply before emailing again. No exceptions. Did Gavin stick to the pattern and take my lack of response to his last message as a sign that I was no longer interested? Would he give up on me so easily? Surely he'd have wondered, after I didn't reply for a whole day— and then another and another—whether his last email went astray. I would have, in his position.

My finger hovers above the "return" key. If I press it, I'll know within seconds.

I can't do it.

I push my chair back from the desk, afraid that I'll press "return" by mistake, before I'm sure I want to.

You don't have to look. Ever. Turn off the computer, go downstairs. Forget about him.

No. I won't take the coward's way out, not this time. I've done that already today, more than once. Despite vowing that I wouldn't, I avoided Elmhirst Road when I went back to school to check on Sophie; I went via Upper Heckencott again, there and back. I did the same both ways when I went to collect Ethan and Sophie at the end of the day, though on each of the four journeys I lied to myself right up until the second before I chickened out.

I slide the wheels of my chair closer to the computer. The eleven asterisks that represent the hidden letters of my password are still sitting there, in the box. My password is "11asterisks." I'm still proud of myself for thinking of that: the password that in attempting to conceal itself does the opposite—reveals itself so brazenly that no one would ever guess.

Wincing, I press the "return" key before I can change my mind.

I gasp when I see my inbox. There are seven unread emails from Gavin. Seven.

Thank you, thank you.

No point pretending this surge of excitement is anything else. Even a talented self-deceiver like me wouldn't swallow that one.

I'd have given up before I wrote the seventh email, however distraught I was. Gavin didn't.

This is it: why I lie, and keep secrets, and take crazy risks—for this feeling. No chemical could give me the same buzz: the thrill of being so wanted, so sought after.

I start to open the messages, one by one. They were all sent within four days of my decision to break off contact with Gavin: four on the first day of my silence and then one on each consecutive day after that.

Hi Nicki, I'm writing to check that my last email to you didn't go astray. Let me know. G.

It's pathetic, isn't it, me worrying because you haven't emailed me for a few hours? Don't want you to think

I can't last a day or even several without hearing from you, but you know what it's like—once a pattern's been established, any disruption to said pattern causes concern. And did you realize that we've emailed each other **at least** twenty times a day since we started? G.

PS—in case you've forgotten when our exchange started, it was 24 February. You made a reference once to deleting all your emails from me, for security. I deliberately kept shtum (not wanting you to think I'm careless about security, which I'm not) and I don't know if you assumed that I delete all your emails after reading too, but I don't. I keep them. I reread them. They mean a lot to me. I hope that's OK with you. That's why I wasn't upset by the idea of you deleting your side of our conversation, because I'm keeping it safe at my end. Don't worry. I promise you no one but me will ever see it. G.

PPS—feelings, eh? They complicate things, don't they? I hope I haven't freaked you out by writing about what can only be described as non-carnal matters. I won't make a habit of it, I promise. Let me know you're OK and aren't sick of me yet, and I'll go back to talking mainly about your nipples, I promise. (Well, I might cover a few other parts of your body, to be fair. In my emails and, in due course, with my own body—I hope.) G.

No, no, no. This is wrong.

I feel dizzy, disorientated. I want and need words from

Gavin, but not these words. This doesn't sound like him. This sounds too much like a real person, someone I might know or be friends with. Gavin has always sounded like . . .

What?

Like something automated. Short toneless sentences, short paragraphs. Like an android giving erotic instructions. The kind of written voice that disembodied words on a screen might have if they had a voice.

And that was exactly what you wanted, wasn't it? What does that say about you?

In due course with his own body? Did he really mean that? Do I want him to mean it?

Gavin and I arranged to meet once, in May, after agreeing we were ready to take things to the next level. Then he had to cancel; he didn't say why. After that, neither of us mentioned rearranging. I didn't mind. Secretly, I was relieved. If we didn't meet, that meant that what I was doing wasn't as bad. If I thought of him as unreal, one-dimensional, a computer program generating words designed to elicit a specific physical response, then I could almost persuade myself that I didn't really have another man in my life, one who wasn't my husband.

Still wrong.

Not as grievously wrong as a physical affair, though. Maybe. And the emails were enough. God, they were so much more than enough: endless, detailed, graphically descriptive orders from a man I'd never met, whose face I'd never seen, not even in a photograph. None of my real-life lovers has ever been so uninhibited in the words he used or the things he asked and expected me to do—and nor was I ever so . . . pornographic, for want of a better word, with any of them. Gavin swept away all my inhibitions by ignoring them completely, refusing to acknowledge they existed and simply repeating his demands. Eventually, I stopped bothering to mention that I was too shy and simply did as I was told.

And loved it. Craved more and more of it.

All I know about Gavin is that he's English, in his mid-forties, married with no children and works from home. That's what he's told me, anyway. I suppose any or all of it might not be true. I didn't and don't really care. All I cared about was the way he made me feel. On two occasions, his insistent explicit words alone were enough to push me over the edge—just the words and my imagination, and not even a brush of a fingertip. No other man has ever had that effect on me.

Not even King Edward.

Whom I swore I wouldn't allow into my mind again. That's why Gavin: to block out King Edward. Amazing, really, how well it worked.

Until now.

I am gasping for breath, though I've done nothing physically strenuous. I grip the desk to steady myself.

Think about Gavin. Not . . . anybody else. Gavin.

The blank tonelessness of his words was an important part of the attraction. So different. And yet three of the four new messages from him that I've just read—all but the first one—don't sound like him at all. Did my abandonment panic him so much that his online persona slipped?

I promise you no one but me will ever see it . . .

I won't make a habit of it, I promise . . .
I'll go back to talking mainly about your nipples, I promise . . .
Feelings, eh?

A shudder rocks my body. I don't want Gavin's feelings or his promises. King Edward gave me feelings and promises, and they counted for nothing in the end. And I don't want amusing banter and wordplay from Gavin either. Adam jokes around. So did King Edward. I love witty men, normally. I mean, I used to.

You still do love Adam. Never forget that.

Gavin has never been funny, warm or affectionate before. It's the reason I felt safe in my dealings with him. I wanted and needed him to be avid but not caring, never emotional. I can't stand to think of him as a vulnerable man whose heart I might have broken.

I don't want to think about him any more today—it's already too much—but I can't log out, not without reading everything.

I open message number five:

Nicki, seriously, are you OK? I'm starting to indulge in paranoid worst-case-scenario delusions here. Has your husband found out about us? Have you found out something about me? Are you in hospital, with no access to email? G.

Nicki? Where are you? G.

Do you want to hear my latest theory? You always sign your emails "N x." I always sign mine "G." You've decided I'm a cold, emotionless husk because I won't sign off with a kiss. That's why you've gone missing from my cyber-life. Right? For your information, I've never signed emails with an "x" and I don't think I ever would, however I felt about someone. It's fine when women do it, but from a man it would look somewhat effeminate, I think. Also, I can't believe this would bother you suddenly when it never has before? Or maybe it has, and you've been waiting and hoping . . . ? Look, I'm a big boy. I can handle honesty. Will you tell me what I've done wrong? G x (just this once, for strategic effect, because . . . well, because I'm rather fond of you, Nicki. Perhaps I should have said so before.)

No. No. This is unbearable.

Kind, sincere, affectionate words. Of all the things to become phobic about. *Fuck you, King Edward. You're to blame for this.*

I'm glad there's no mirror in this room. I would hate to see what I look like.

A disaster area. There's not a person on the planet who wouldn't be better off without you in their lives, not even your children.

Instead of shutting the computer down and running away, I force myself to read all seven of Gavin's emails again—not once but several times. By the time I've finished, the words seem less threatening and my hands have stopped shaking.

How can he care about me this much? He barely knows me. Correction: he doesn't know me at all.

And yet, not knowing him either, I care about him too. The way he rescued me from the brink . . .

Far from objecting to it, I like the little dot he always puts after his initial. I like his vulgar email address, mr_jugs@ hushmail.com, and his habit of putting two asterisks on either side of a word or group of words to convey insistence.

Have you found out something about me? What did he mean by that?

What should I do?

No one to ask, or answer, apart from myself. At one time, I'd have told Melissa. I told her everything, before she resigned from her position as my confidante.

There is no one I can think of—not one single person in my life—who would be interested in discussing the changeable writing style of a man who goes by the name of "Mr. Jugs" in order to seek anonymous physical gratification online.

If I ever did muster the courage to tell anybody, I would get no useful analysis, and plenty of soul--destroying condemnation: from my female friends, my brother, my parents; from Adam, assuming he'd speak to me ever again if he knew the truth, and not simply throw me out on the street in horror. And—-though I hate to think about it—I would get shock and disgust from Sophie and Ethan too. They might only be ten and eight, but they understand what betrayal is even if they wouldn't use the word.

My children. Who are downstairs. Who believe I'm looking after them because all three of us are in the house at the same time and I'm the adult.

Tears fill my eyes as a violent internal current sweeps my

breath away. This used to happen a lot before I stopped emailing Gavin, often when I was sitting here, in front of the computer screen: a sudden flood of realization that something terrible is happening—something precious is being irrevocably destroyed—and, though it's my fault, I can't stop it. I have no control.

Four or five seconds later, my eyes are dry, and I can breathe easily. I couldn't recreate the doomed feeling if I tried; it's as if it never happened.

I press my eyes shut so that I can't see the computer in front of me, and wish that the Internet had never been invented. I tell myself that I absolutely mustn't—must not—email Gavin, for the sake of my family, but instead of hearing my own voice saying the words, I hear Melissa's, which blend with the sand-haired policeman's, though neither of them has ever said those words to me.

Their judgment, though I've conjured it out of nowhere, is too heavy a burden to bear. I can only escape if I defy it outright.

I should reread Gavin's messages once more before writing to him—allow their significance to sink in. There might be something I've missed . . .

No. No time. Adam will be home any minute. And Gavin has waited long enough to hear from me. I might still matter to him as much as I did when he sent those emails; by tomorrow, he might have stopped caring. I don't want to leave it too late.

I open his most recent message and press "reply." My fingers are numb, unreliable. It takes me three attempts to manage "Hi Gavin" without typos. Then I delete it and write, "Dear Gavin," instead. "Hi" is too casual.

> *I'm so sorry I haven't replied before now. Until today, I haven't opened my hushmail account for more than three weeks. I decided I couldn't do what we were doing any more. It was nothing you did wrong, so please don't worry about that. I don't want to go into detail, but I had a minor skirmish with the police that was kind of linked to my involvement with you. It shook me up and I lost what little courage I had. I decided we had to stop before something irreversible happened. In an ideal world, I would love for us to be in touch again. You saved my sanity and brought unexpected pleasure into the darkest patch of my life. But it's just not possible. Once again, I'm so sorry. I wish you all the very best. N x*

I press "send," wiping away my tears with my other hand. There. I've done the right thing for once. I'm glad the urge to behave honorably doesn't seize me more often if this is how it feels: like hollowing out my heart and stuffing it full of grayness.

The darkest patch of my life. Was that an over-the-top way to put it?

In February, thanks to King Edward—King Edward VII, to give him his full alias—I considered taking my own life. For a few days I wasn't sure that even the thought of Sophie and Ethan, motherless, would be enough to persuade me to stay in this world.

I'm about to sign out of Hushmail when a new message appears in the inbox.

Gavin. Oh God. Christ, God. Of course it's him: no one else knows I have this email address. I used to hushmail King Edward from a Gmail account. I didn't know email existed until I answered Gavin's advertisement and he wrote back from a Hushmail account.

How has he managed to reply so quickly? Has he been sitting in front of his computer for three weeks and four days, waiting?

I hope he hasn't. Almost as much as I hope he has.

I try to grasp the mouse, aim wrong and knock it off the table. Having restored it to its place on the mat, I take a deep breath and click to open the message.

It's one line long:

More detail about your encounter with the police, please. G.

I type an equally short response:

No. It was horrendous. I want to forget it ever happened.

I don't sign off with my usual "N x." I hope this is a tactful way of demonstrating that we are no longer an item, insofar as we ever were. My replying doesn't mean I've entered back into a correspondence with him, and this exchange has nothing to do with sex. He's just being nosey; as soon as he sees that it won't work, he'll give up.

Another new Hushmail appears in my inbox. I open it.

All right, so you had a brush with the police and decided you couldn't write to me any more—fair enough (or I'm sure it would be, if I understood why). So what changed today? Did they only just let you out of jail? G.

I smile in spite of myself.

So, Gavin turns out to have a sense of humor. Is that so bad? Not all charming, funny men are evil. Adam, for example.

My fingers hover over the keyboard. I want to answer, but how can I justify responding a second time if I really want to break this off?

Does Gavin think that if he puts nothing sexual in his messages, I'll decide it's OK to write to him?

If we're not going to do the cyber-sex thing, what's in it for him? Or for me?

I don't want him as a platonic friend. That would be awful. If I have to choose between types of loss—and it appears that I do—I'd rather have the sudden dizzying kind, not a long-drawn-out diminishment.

I type:

No jail. I saw the same policeman again today. It reminded me that it was because of him that I'd stopped writing to you. I decided I owed you an explanation. That's all. Please stop emailing me. I don't want to be your pen pal. All or nothing for me, and it has to be nothing. Again, I'm so sorry. N x

I press "send."

All done.

Log out, Nicki. Why are you still sitting here, staring at your inbox? How devastated will you be if he doesn't write back immediately?

Then why did you order him not to?

His reply arrives within seconds.

I agree: you owe me an explanation. What happened with the policeman? First time and second time, please. All or nothing is a sound principle—and since you've already given me some of the story, you must now supply all of it. G.

This sounds more like the Gavin I'm familiar with: wooden. Giving me orders. Desire stirs inside me. I shift in my chair.

Should I tell him? If I don't, he'll never understand, not really. Can I bring myself to write what happened in an email? The prospect makes my skin prickle.

I click on "reply." Downstairs, a door bangs shut, making me jump.

"Kids!" I call out. "Don't slam the door!"

"Not kids. Me. Sorry."

Adam. *Shit.*

Terror floods my body, freezing me in place. It's a few seconds before I can move again. I grab the mouse. "I'll be down in a sec," I shout. *Please don't come upstairs.*

What will Adam do? I listen for clues, with the cursor

hovering over 'Sign Out' in the top right-hand corner of the screen. *Please go into the kitchen, Adam. I need a few more seconds . . .*

I hear the creak of a door—the living room, I'm guessing—followed by Adam trying unsuccessfully to talk to the children. He gives up after a minute or so. I hold my breath, listening for footsteps on the stairs.

Nothing. He must have gone into the kitchen, or to the bathroom.

You don't know that. Sign out. Don't risk it.

I type:

Need to go now. Might explain later. No promises, though. Bye. N x

I press "send," then sign out. Then I go to "History," click on "Show All History" and delete all the email entries. I'm so grateful that I can do this. It's the online equivalent of saying a few Hail Marys and being absolved of all your sins. *Thank you, technology.*

What next? I can't think straight. Oh yes, I know: Yahoo Mail, my respectable email account.

Adam pushes open the spare-room door as I'm opening a message from my mum. "Hi, hon," he says. "OK day?"

"Brilliant, thanks," I tell him. "You?"

"Why brilliant?"

"Well, actually . . . not *that* brilliant." *Come on, Brain, start working, for fuck's sake.* I have nothing to be excited about, not officially. I must keep this in mind—for the rest of my life, ideally.

It's a good sign that, after only three weeks and four days of being good, I am already much worse at lying.

I'm not going to start lying to Adam again. I can't.

"I had to go to school and back four times," I say. The email from my mother about when we're next all going to get together is still up on the screen. Not at all secret from my husband, but still . . . I ought to feel more guilty about this ongoing correspondence than I do about the one with Gavin.

If I'm making a list of people to cut off contact with, my parents have surely earned their place at the top.

You're not cutting anyone off, though, are you? You never will.

How did I not hear Adam on the stairs? He could so easily have caught me.

But he didn't.

Being bad and getting away with it: there's no feeling like it.

About the Author

SOPHIE HANNAH is the *New York Times* bestselling author of nine psychological thrillers as well as *The Monogram Murders*, the first novel to be authorized by the estate of Agatha Christie. Her books have received numerous awards, including the UK National Book Award, and are published in twenty-seven countries. She lives in Cambridge, England.

Discover great authors, exclusive offers, and more at hc.com.